CRIME THROUGH TIME™

ICED!

BILL DOYLE

CRIME THROUGH TIME™

ICED!

THE 2007 JOURNAL OF NICK FITZMORGAN

LITTLE, BROWN AND COMPANY
New York Boston

Cover illustration by Steve Cieslawski
Interior illustrations by Philomena Simpson
Back cover and title page illustration by Brian Dow
Designed by Atif Toor and Mark Weinberg
Photos: p. 11/Library of Congress; pp. 33, 71/Ablestock; p. 52/Laura Miller; p. 55/L. C. Casterline; p. 135/Riccardo Salmona
The Inspector photos: p. 1 (top) Corbis, (bottom) L. C. Casterline; p. 2 (top) Ablestock, (bottom) KRT/Newscom; p. 3 (top) PR Newswire Photo Service/Newscom; (center right) Mario Ruiz/Zuma Press/Newscom; p. 4 (top right) Worth Conoy/Icon SMI/Newscom, (top left) L. C. Casterline, (center left) PR Newswire Photo Service/Newscom

Developed by Nancy Hall, Inc.

Little, Brown and Company
Hachette Book Group USA
1271 Avenue of the Americas, New York, NY 10020
Visit our Web site at www.lb-kids.com

First Edition: September 2006

Library of Congress Cataloging-in-Publication Data

Doyle, Bill H., 1968–
Iced! : the 2007 journal of Nick Fitzmorgan.—1st ed.
p. cm. — (Crime through time)
Summary: In 2007, fourteen-year-old Nick Fitzmorgan arrives home to find that his father has disappeared but has left clues, including blood on an MP-3 player and goofy song lyrics, that lead the young detective all the way to Mount Everest.
ISBN-13: 978-0-316-05753-0 (trade pbk.)
ISBN-10: 0-316-05753-3 (trade pbk.)
[1. Mountaineering—Fiction. 2. Everest, Mount (China and Nepal)—Fiction. 3. Mystery and detective stories.] I. Title.
PZ7.D7725Ice 2006
[Fic]—dc22 2005027306

10 9 8 7 6 5 4 3 2 1

CW

Printed in the United States of America

ACKNOWLEDGMENTS

A thank-you of historic proportions to Nancy Hall for making this book and the Crime Through Time series a reality. To Kirsten Hall for her insightful grasp of the overall picture, to Linda Falken for her skillful editing and amazing eagle-eye for detail, and to Atif Toor for bringing the books alive visually.

Special thanks to the editors at Little, Brown: Andrea Spooner, Jennifer Hunt, Phoebe Sorkin, and Rebekah Rush McKay, who are always dead-on, always incisive, and never discouraging. And thanks to Riccardo Salmona for his constant support.

THE SWAMP

June 2, 2007

12:30 PM

I felt something slimy curl around my ankle—and I froze.

Insects buzzed around my head, and the surrounding swamp gave off the sickening smell of rotten eggs. But I forced myself to stay still. My legs were submerged in waist-high water, thick with muck. I had no idea what creature had wrapped itself around my leg, and I didn't want to startle it. For all I knew, it could be a friendly little snake—or it could be an angry cottonmouth with really sharp fangs and dangerous venom. After a few tense moments under the sweltering sun, I felt the creature uncoil. There was a tiny ripple on the grayish-brown surface as it slithered away.

I continued wading through the gunk, forcing myself not to hurry even though that unplanned stop might have cost me the mission.

This morning, I had been given specific instructions to trail the Suspect—and to do so without being spotted. Losing him in the swamp would mean failure, and failure isn't something I handle so well.

Around me, the swamp gurgled like something out of an old horror movie. Dead tree trunks sprouted up here and there. To my left, the swamp was edged by massive weeping willows that blocked the sight of the nearby dirt road.

Could the Suspect have gone that way? I wondered.

As if to answer me, I heard the snap of a twig coming from the direction of the trees.

June 2, 2007

I ducked behind a hollowed-out tree trunk. I was just about to risk peering through a hole in the rotted trunk—when a hand reached through and grabbed my shoulder. I jumped and let out a little yell.

The hand released me. I looked through the hole and saw a pair of reflective sunglasses staring back at me. They were worn by a guy who was in his late twenties and had a face like a bulldog. He had a crew cut so short it made him look almost bald, and he was a wearing a dark suit.

"Judge Pinkerton would like to see you," Mr. Bulldog said in a gravelly voice.

I shook myself free of his hand and walked around to his side of the tree. Mr. Bulldog—a nickname the students had given him—was one of the top detectives at the facility and an ace at moving with stealth. No wonder I hadn't heard him. "I'm on a training mission," I told him.

"It's been terminated," he growled.

My stomach sank in disappointment. "But what about the Suspect?"

"Your training partner has been informed," Mr. Bulldog replied over his shoulder. He was already walking back toward the dirt road, knowing that I would follow. No one at the training facility would ignore a summons from Judge Pinkerton.

Passing through the line of trees, I found Mr. Bulldog sitting in the driver's seat of a souped-up golf cart, which was part ATV, part lunar rover. The huge, balloon-like wheels and the flexible axles could handle the rocky terrain in the area. The cart could cruise easily over fallen trees that might block the road.

After shaking off as much of the muck from my jeans as I could, I hopped into the passenger seat. Mr. Bulldog drove us along the dirt road that wound its way through the 600-acre Private Detective Academy. Spread over a landscape of mountains, forests, clearings, and a swamp, PDA was like a small town.

But to live in this town, you had to want to be a detective—and you had to be eighteen or older. Of course, that isn't true in my case. I just turned fourteen last month. Judge Pinkerton, who started PDA, had made an exception in my case and let me attend a special four-week training program.

For the past three weeks, I'd been part of a kind of detective boot camp. Each day started at six in the morning with a four-mile run, followed by training exercises, classroom instruction—including stuff on forensics (my favorite!)—and more training exercises.

Not exactly what most kids would do on summer break, but I was happier than I could remember. Even though at first, my chest had burned during the outdoor training.

June 2, 2007

Surrounded by mountains, PDA was several thousand feet above sea level, and my lungs had struggled to suck oxygen out of the high-altitude air. But after a few days, I'd made the adjustment.

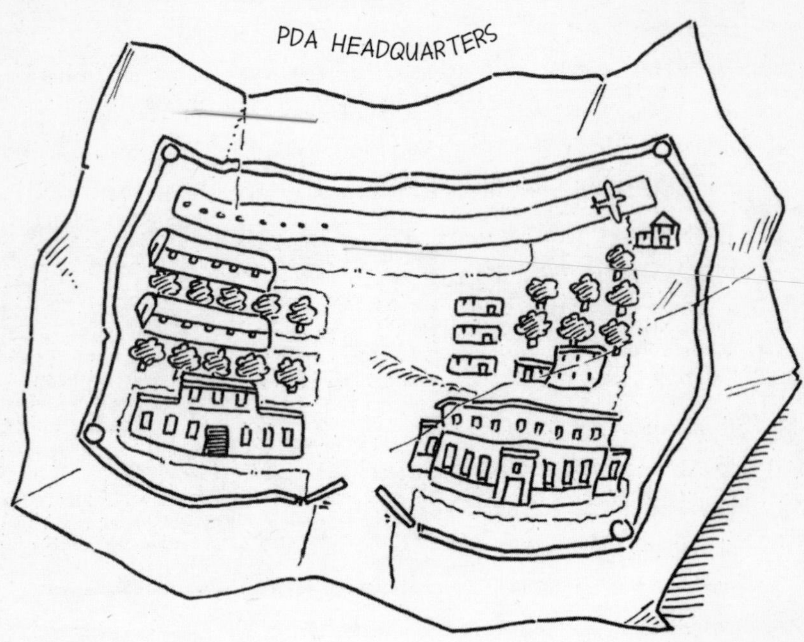

To my surprise, we didn't go back to the main building that held the facility's offices. Instead, we headed in the opposite direction, straight to the private airstrip. There, I spotted a sleek Learjet on the tarmac, its idling engines whining.

We pulled up next to the plane. Judge Pinkerton stood waiting for us, her purple silk scarf and silver hair blowing in the breeze. Judge was an old friend of both the Fitz-morgans and the Moories, the two branches of my family.

WORLD'S FIRST PRIVATE EYE

Allan Pinkerton was born in Glasgow, Scotland. In 1842, he immigrated to the United States, where he settled in Chicago, Illinois. After helping round up a gang of counterfeiters, Pinkerton became a deputy sheriff and then Chicago's first detective. In 1850, he founded the first private detective agency and, while working for a railroad company, he became friends with attorney Abraham Lincoln. In 1860, it was Pinkerton who prevented president-elect Lincoln from being assassinated. At Lincoln's request, Pinkerton formed a secret service to spy on the South for the Union.

JUDGE IS A PINKERTON!

Looking at Judge, it's easy to forget that she's over a hundred years old. Her back is still straight and she's nearly six feet tall. Unlike other older people I know, the skin on her face didn't sag with age. It just thinned slightly and grew tighter over her high cheekbones. The only heavy wrinkles were the laugh lines around her mouth and eyes. Judge used a cane made of strong drift-wood, a gift from Uncle Mal, but she could still get around pretty well. And her bright blue eyes had never lost their intensity.

Now those eyes were burning more brightly than ever. "Nick, thanks for coming so quickly," she said as I hopped out of the cart and walked over to her.

"Hi, Judge. What's up?" I expected her to present me with another challenging mission.

"I'm sorry, Nick," she said. "I'm going to have to cut your training short."

I was stunned. "What?"

"I'm sending you home." She must have seen the concern on my face because she held up a hand before I could speak. "No, don't worry. Nothing's wrong with your dad. Henry is fine."

That was a relief. But it didn't answer any of the other questions that suddenly flooded my mind. "Then what's the problem, Judge?"

She didn't answer. Instead, she signaled to Mr. Bulldog, who strode over to us. He carried my green duffel bag in one hand and my journal in the other. Normally, I keep this journal on me at all times, but I knew we'd be getting wet in today's training and didn't want to take the chance of dropping it in the swamp.

Mr. Bulldog handed me my things and went back to the cart.

"What is going on?" I asked.

"Speed is of the essence, my friend," Judge said. "So I asked my aide to grab your belongings on his way to pick you up. You can change into a clean pair of jeans on the plane." Before I could say anything, she continued, "My pilot, Maura, will fly you to Hanahan Airport outside Los Angeles."

I turned to see a young woman—almost a girl—standing at the top of the steps leading up to the plane's doorway. She must have been inside when I arrived. About nineteen, she was athletic looking and wore a sleek, dark suit over an immaculate white shirt. Her red hair was cut short and her angular face was dusted with freckles. But this sweet face was set in an all-business expression.

MAURA, THE PILOT

"Please make sure Nick gets home safely," Judge instructed. The pilot nodded curtly and disappeared back into the plane.

"She seems friendly," I joked under my breath.

Judge smiled. "Maura was top in her class here and is my best pilot. And you two have more in common than you might think." She patted my arm. "Go on, now."

This was unbelievable! She was sending me away without an explanation. I felt a flash of frustration. "Why did you spend three weeks training me if you won't let me help when something's wrong?" I asked.

"Nothing's wrong, Nick," Judge replied.

The skin at the base of my neck prickled as I looked at Judge's face. My detective radar was running at full blast.

Tec tip

FROM ESME HUNTER'S DETECTIVE HANDBOOK

THE BODY LANGUAGE OF LIARS

LOST YOUR LIE DETECTOR? NOT TO WORRY! ONE OR MORE OF THE SIGNS LISTED BELOW COULD INDICATE YOUR SUBJECT IS LYING. CHECK TO SEE IF HE OR SHE IS...

- Blushing or showing patchy red spots on the face
- Avoiding eye contact
- Rubbing the back of the neck
- Involuntarily shrugging the shoulders
- Speaking with a shaky voice
- Showing facial or muscle twitching
- Sweating even when the air is cool

Ever since I can remember, I've had the ability to "read" people. My dad and Judge are always joking that I'm like a walking lie detector.

At the orphanage where I spent the first seven years of my life, I could tell in a fraction of a second whether or not potential parents were thinking about taking me home. My senses naturally zoomed in on a person's facial expressions, changes in body language, and even the way they talked. Each time, I was correct.

My perfect record continued when Henry Fitzmorgan walked through the door of the orphanage with Judge Pinkerton by his side. I knew at that exact second that I had spotted my new family.

And that's why watching her face now, I knew Judge wasn't telling me the truth. Something was definitely wrong.

But she wasn't sharing.

Fine, I thought, trying not to pout. She must have her reasons for being secretive. "Okay, thanks for everything," I said and hefted the duffel over my shoulder. I started up the steps to the plane, my mucky sneakers squishing. "See you later."

"Wait," Judge suddenly called after me. I turned back and saw she had moved closer to the stairs. "Forgive me, Nick. You're old enough to be told what's happening."

"Thanks, Judge," I said, feeling instantly better.

But her face remained grave. "Have you heard about the Notabe case I've been working on?"

I nodded. Everyone in my family knew about the Notabe case.

Asyla Notabe, a wealthy woman who had recently tripled her fortune by investing in a cloning program, had been in and out of the lives of my family and Judge for about

ASYLA NOTABE

a century. Whenever Asyla appeared, trouble would follow. Lately, Asyla had made it her quest to convince the government to ban private investigators. She argued that because PI's worked for private people, they could be hired as a private army. She said they were dangerous to national security.

It turns out Asyla might be the true threat. Judge had caught her passing bribes to elected officials. Asyla had been trying to buy votes so that her "anti-private detective" bill would pass.

Now Judge was saying, "There are a few loose ends I need to tie up to make sure Asyla's trial goes well. It's something I hadn't expected. My work will take me away from PDA, and I'll be out of touch for the next week."

"You mean you're going undercover?" I asked.

"Yes," she said. A sudden smile lit up her face. "Even we old people still like to get out in the field." Then, more seriously, she added, "I won't able to oversee your training here as we'd planned. But we'll complete your courses at another time, okay?"

I nodded. I didn't like leaving, but at least she was being straight with me. "I'm glad you told me the truth, Judge," I said.

"Your radar wouldn't allow anything less." She reached out and tousled my hair. "I spoke to your dad early this morning. I told him what an amazing job you've done here and that you'd be home later today. I'll contact him again to let him know your exact time of arrival."

"I'll call him from the plane," I said. "You've got enough going on."

Judge's bright blue eyes searched mine. "So are we okay?"

Before answering, I took a few more steps up toward the airplane door. Then I turned and said with a smile, "Always, Judge."

She beamed at me. "Bully for you, Nick!"

MAURA TALKING TO THE LIMO DRIVER

June 2, 2007

4:30 PM

A long black car picked us up at the private airport outside of Los Angeles. The squat driver showed us his PDA badge, and Maura said a few words to him. I tossed my bag in the trunk and hopped in the backseat. When Maura climbed in next to me, I said, "I'm okay. You don't need to take me to my house."

Maura gave me a cool look that could have frozen the sun. "Judge Pinkerton told me to take you home."

"Did I mention she also said you should buy me a new big-screen HDTV?" I asked.

Sure, it was a dumb joke, but Maura's expression didn't change at all. I wondered if she had ever smiled in her life.

I had tried calling my dad from the airplane. But I hadn't been able to get through to either our home phone or his cell. There had been two or three rings, and then a strange click followed by a high-pitched buzzing. Must've been some kind of interference from the plane's phone.

I thought about asking to borrow Maura's cell phone but wasn't sure how she felt about sharing. Besides, I was almost home. I might as well just surprise Dad with my early return.

During the forty-five minute ride to my house, Maura sat ramrod straight. I was glad she didn't feel like she had to make chitchat. I'm not so good at that and find it even more exhausting than a 4-mile run in the mountains.

The car wound its way through the twisty streets of my neighborhood in the Hollywood Hills. We pulled up in front of my one-story house. The sight of the curving stone walk and my dad's brightly colored flower garden made me realize that I had really missed this place—and my dad.

Maura coolly scanned the little house. "I'll ask the driver to wait until you open the front door."

"Okay," I agreed. "Bye, then."

She nodded. I grabbed my things and got out of the car. Feeling Maura's eyes on me, I walked to the front porch, unlocked the door, and opened it. I gave her a wave, and the car sped off down the street.

Gee, nothing like a teary good-bye, I thought as I went inside.

"Hi, Dad!" I shouted. "Your favorite son is home!"

MOM AND DAD

That's our little joke. Actually, I'm his only son.

Like everyone else in my family, my dad is a detective. He turned one of his most famous cases—the one about that serial bank robber in Florida—into a script. The script was turned into a hit movie that won an Oscar. Ever since then my dad has been writing scripts, turning true mysteries into exciting movies.

Dad's life hasn't always been like a happy Hollywood ending, though. His wife died ten years ago, and he grieved for her for a long time. He always says Judge was the one who got him through that tough time.

Three years after his wife passed away, he adopted me. I was just seven at the time. Now, it is just the pair of us in the house. We've become extremely close and share a stronger bond than most biological sons and fathers.

And I'd be the first one to say: That's no small thing. Spending time in the orphanage didn't exactly help me learn to trust people. But it made me extremely independent. I think that self-reliance helps make me such a strong detective.

"Hello!" I called, dumping my bag in the front hall. Once again, there was no response. "Dad, your welcome is less than overwhelming!"

Sometimes when Dad gets involved in writing, even an earthquake couldn't bring him out of his imaginary world. And I knew he was really into his latest project, some script about world explorers.

I made my way to the snug little kitchen, which Dad and I had painted bright red together. There had been plenty of food on the plane, but I'm always hungry. I had just constructed the world's most perfect roast-beef sandwich, when—DING-DONG!

"Door!" I shouted. When there was no answer from Dad, I reluctantly left my beautiful sandwich and headed back to the front door.

Must be Uncle Benny, I thought. Benny was the producer of Dad's first movie and they've worked together on other films since then. They became such close friends that my dad made him my godfather.

June 2, 2007

He's always showing up at the house right around this time of day, saying that he's got "business" to discuss. But I think it's just to see what we've got grilling in the backyard.

Benny is a good-looking blonde guy, the tall, lanky type who looks like he'd be a great tennis player. His fast-talking style makes lots of people crazy. It's like trying to chat with a hyper Chihuahua that's had way too much coffee. But I know he means well.

KID—
EVERYONE NEEDS A GODFATHER. SO I SHOWED UP A LITTLE LATE IN YOUR LIFE. THAT MEANS I'VE GOT A LOT OF MAKING UP TO DO, THAT'S ALL — Benny

When I opened the door, my godfather wasn't standing there. Instead, there was a dark-haired man who wore a thick, brown coat made of scratchy-looking material. He had a fur-lined hat on top of his head and a birthmark under his right eye. Just from the way he stood, I could tell he wasn't more than twenty years old. But the golden skin on his face looked like he'd spent a lot of time outdoors.

"Can I help—?" I started to say.

"Wonefas nepo!" he shouted in a deep, scratchy voice.

Whoa. I took a step back into the hall. This is why they warn you to look through the peephole before opening the door.

"Wonefas nepo!" the man repeated.

THE MYSTERIOUS DARK-HAIRED MAN

I took Chinese and German in school, but this wasn't like any language I had heard before.

I looked to see if my neighbors were around, in case I needed help. The street was empty. "What?" I said to the man. "I'm sorry, I don't know what—"

"Wonefas nepo!" he shouted again. This time he emphasized his strange words by tossing something white with a rounded top at me.

Instinctively, my hands flew up and caught it before it could smash on the tile of the hall. My mouth opened in shock as I looked down at the smooth object I now held.

It was a human skull!

Before I could utter another sound, the strange man suddenly turned and rushed off the porch. I heard a tearing sound as his jacket snagged a large splinter on one of the wooden pillars. He raced across the lawn and disappeared down the sidewalk.

HE THREW A SKULL AT ME AND RAN!

Finally, my shock had subsided enough for my mouth to work again. Holding up the skull like he had just dropped off a housewarming present, I called after him, "Thanks!"

I figured he must be one of Dad's kooky Hollywood friends pulling some kind of prank. But then again . . .

Automatically, I went to the kitchen and pulled out a clean plastic bag from the drawer. Returning to the porch,

I carefully removed the fabric, put it in the baggie, and sealed it tight. Once back inside with the door closed, I put the bag safely into my jacket pocket.

As I did this, I caught sight of myself in the foyer mirror. I realized this was probably a strange reaction to someone ripping his coat. But I guess it's what happens when you grow up in a family of detectives.

Tec Tip

FROM ESME HUNTER'S DETECTIVE HANDBOOK

HAIR TODAY, GONE TOMORROW?

WHEN COLLECTING HAIR AND FIBERS (LIKE PIECES OF CLOTHING) AT A CRIME SCENE, JUST REMEMBER HAIR:

Hunt thoroughly around the scene—this evidence can be tiny and hard to find!

Acquire the sample carefully—don't mix up your own hair with the evidence

Isolate the hair or fiber in a sealed envelope or plastic bag

Retain the sample in a safe place until you're ready to examine it

Lugging a skull around the house might also sound strange to most people. But for me, it wasn't all that weird. Last year, Aunt Tonia pulled some strings. She's a medical examiner and got UCLA to let me sit in on several courses on facial reconstruction. Even if I hadn't aced the classes, I'd have known this wasn't a real skull anyway. It was just a very good plaster replica.

June 2, 2007

I walked down the hallway that leads away from the kitchen and stopped outside the office I share with my dad. I held the skull through the door. "Hello? I'm looking for any BODY," I called in a creepy voice, like it was the skull talking.

But when I didn't hear Dad's usual chuckle, I walked in and found the room empty.

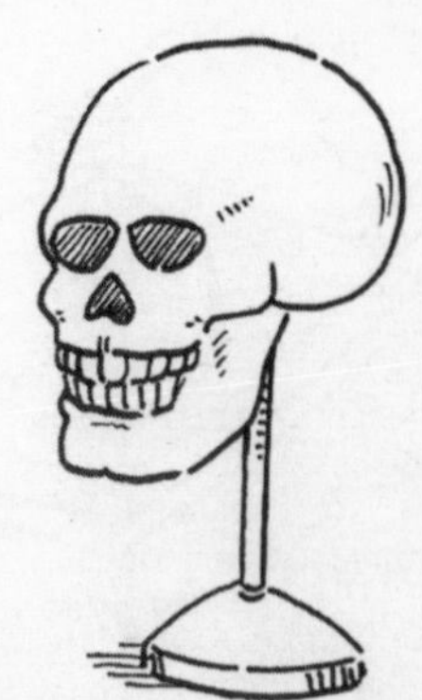

I put the replica of the skull carefully on my work stand, a 2-foot-long pole with a sturdy base and a clamp at the top. I gently turned the screw to tighten the clamp around the back of the cranium—exactly the way I do every time I'm working on a skull.

I looked around the office to see if Dad had left me a note. The room was the largest one in the house. It used to be a two-car garage before my dad and I put down some green carpet and turned it into our office. He writes and works on his cases on one side, and I have my desk on the other. We'd blown up pictures of us from our trips around the world—like to Rome and Easter Island—and they hung on the walls between the bookshelves.

My dad hadn't written me a note, but he'd sure left a huge mess behind. Papers, books, a stapler, his goldfish bowl full of quarters—things were scattered everywhere.

Grabbing my digital camera, I stood on a chair and snapped a shot of the chaos. I could use this "evidence" if he ever accused me of being the only slob in the family.

I was climbing down when I spotted something unsettling. We had left the three long, rectangular-shaped windows in the garage door that served as one wall of the office. The light streaming through these windows was creating a dull glimmer on the small MP3 player on Dad's desk.

This glimmer of light didn't look quite right . . .

THERE WAS BLOOD ON THE MP3 PLAYER!

I walked closer and leaned in toward the MP3 player. On one corner was a large drop of blood, about the size of penny.

My own blood ran cold.

WHAT WAS GOING ON?

I picked up a pen from Dad's desk and pressed the MP3 play button with it—not wanting to disturb any fingerprints. (Another detective's habit!)

The room filled with singing. Well, some people might consider it singing—but I'd put it right up there with the sound of fingernails scratching down a chalkboard.

It was my dad. And he was belting out strange words in his out-of-tune voice. The refrain of the song went like this:

I shutter to think when life envelops
All that my clicking bug could develop.

Even with all this really weird stuff happening, I felt my face flush. It's embarrassing, but Dad calls me "Bug" sometimes as a nickname.

He sang the same lines over and over, and then the song ended.

What the heck was going on? If the lyrics were some kind of clue, they weren't making any sense to me.

I turned my attention back to the drop of blood. Maybe this would give me more answers than that strange song. The first thing I needed to do was figure out who the blood belonged to.

My dad's detective work meant that we had lots of cool gizmos and high-tech investigation equipment around. One of those pieces of equipment was a minilab for DNA matching.

We had practiced using the minilab in one of my college classes a few months ago. Each of us plucked a hair from our head—making sure to get as much of the root as possible. Then we'd used the minilab to create a DNA readout.

Returning to the office, I found Dad's evidence-collecting kit in a dark briefcase in the corner. I took out a pair of plastic gloves and put them on. Then, after removing a clean slide from the kit, I walked over to the MP3 player. By pressing the top of the slide against the drop of blood, I was able to get a small sample to stick to the glass surface.

Dear Dr. DNA:

Q: *I just heard that experts used DNA to solve a thirty-year-old mystery. Tell me about the case.*

A: You have to be more specific! Solving old cases using DNA is happening more and more often. The FBI has collected about 120,000 DNA samples from crime scenes. A computer compares those to a database of 2,700,000 DNA samples from known criminals. If a sample from the scene matches one from a criminal—the FBI knows they've got their crook!

Blood never makes me squeamish, but the thought that I could be handling a drop of my dad's blood—and that he might have been hurt somehow—made my hands shake.

The slide fumbled from my fingers—

"No!" I gasped.

—and went flying across the room.

The glass slide narrowly missed the hard surface of the desk and skittered across the floor. Most of the blood splattered into tiny droplets and soaked into the dark carpet.

I stood horror-struck for a moment. Had I just blown the case? How would I ever match the blood now?

I rushed over and carefully picked up the slide. A very tiny droplet clung to the glass. Things might still work out okay, I thought.

A few years ago, this tiny amount of blood wouldn't be enough to run a DNA analysis. But with recent advances, all that has changed.

BURGLARS BEWARE!

In New York City, only twenty percent of stolen property cases were being solved. But that may soon change, thanks to new DNA testing methods. In the past, experts needed 150 cells' worth of DNA to make a match. Often, burglars don't leave behind that much DNA. Today, only about six cells' worth of DNA are needed for testing, and that small an amount can be found in a smudge of blood or even in a fingerprint.

New York City Bulletin, Spring 2006

Luckily, I was able to get a DNA profile from the remaining droplet of blood. And when I compared it to my dad's profile that we'd made a few months ago, I knew that I had a match.

Now I was certain about two things. The drop of blood had come from my dad. And this was definitely not a game.

After this is all over, I have to thank this guy!

please come to a dinner
in honor of
alec jeffreys,
the father of DNA fingerprinting!

one morning in 1984, the idea hit him like a lightning bolt—and by the afternoon, he had figured out how to use DNA fingerprinting to solve crimes. just a year later, his idea was used to free a person wrongly accused of a crime.

Dad could be in serious danger. He might have struggled when kidnappers took him out of this room. But if he was kidnapped, where was the ransom note?

Nothing made sense!

It was time to call for help.

I went to my dad's desk and hit the speed dial on the videophone. After three rings, Judge's face filled the screen. I could see a wall of her office in the background.

I breathed a sigh of relief.

"Judge, I'm so glad I caught you."

"I'm just leaving now," she said. Seeing my worried look, her eyes narrowed. "Nick, what's wrong? Is your father there?"

"No," I said. "That's why I'm calling. I think Dad might be missing."

Judge looked startled for a moment but then snapped into her all-business mode. "Tell me everything."

I quickly filled her in on the strange man with the skull, the drop of blood, the song—everything that had happened since I arrived home. Judge nodded and asked me questions as I told her.

By the time I finished, Judge already had a plan. "Maura's one of the most sensible people I know. I'm going to call her now and ask her to join you," she said. "This is more than likely just a big misunderstanding, but better safe than sorry."

I asked, "What about the police?"

Judge took a breath. "Normally I would tell you to call them immediately. But the Notabe case I'm wrapping up involves some pretty powerful people in law enforcement, and some of them have taken bribes from her. Maura is the nearest person to you I can trust. She'll be able to help you with everything. In the meantime, use what I taught you here and do what you do best. Put together the pieces of the puzzle."

I heard a voice call out to Judge. It sounded like Mr. Bulldog telling her that they were running late. Judge's eyes never left mine. "Nick, look for Maura," she instructed. "But be careful whom you trust. At least for now. All right?"

"Okay, Judge."

"I'm sure this will all work out, and you'll see your dad soon. I'll be back in touch the second I finish with the Notabe case."

We said our good-byes, and the screen went dark.

I looked around the office. I felt better after talking with Judge, but was still pretty much at a loss. What could I do to help track down my dad?

"Put together the pieces of the puzzle," Judge Pinkerton had told me on the phone.

But how could I do that if I couldn't even find the pieces? I felt as empty-headed as the skull.

The piece of cloth from the strange man's coat! The skull! They must be clues. I followed my instincts. First, the cloth. It would be faster. When I pulled it out of the baggie, I saw that there were several hairs stuck to it.

I did a quick hair/fiber analysis. The hairs didn't match any of the human samples on my database. But then I was struck by a thought. What if the hair hadn't come from a person—but from an animal?

Tec tip

FROM ESME HUNTER'S DETECTIVE HANDBOOK

HAIR AND FIBER ANALYSIS

Under a microscope, it can be determined whether or not a hair or fiber is from a human. Once the determination has been made that it's not human, there are four choices of what it can be: mineral, vegetable, animal, or synthetic. Once the hair or fiber has been narrowed down to one of these four groups, it can be compared with other known samples, and a match can be determined.

I tapped into the Museum of Natural History's computer and discovered that the hair had come from a yak. And what was more interesting was that the follicle was still attached.

This fact meant that the hair came directly from a yak and had not been processed into a shirt or something. One of the only ways this hair could have gotten on the strange man would be if he had recently been at a yak farm—or, I thought dryly, a petting zoo with yaks.

Now for the skull. Tearing a page from my forensic anthropology textbook, I got to work.

USING CLAY IN FACIAL RECONSTRUCTION

STEP 1: Try to determine the sex of the person and age at time of death. For age, examine teeth. For gender, look at three points: bone at lower back of skull, ridge above eyes, bone below ear—these areas are larger in males.

STEP 2: Attach 20 to 35 pegs to show the thickness of flesh the average person has in those spots.

STEP 3: Insert plastic balls for eyes. Using pegs as guides, place clay "flesh" on the skull to form facial muscles.

STEP 4: Shape the nose. There are no bones to guide you, so use your best judgment. Fill in the rest of the face with clay until the tops of the pegs are covered.

STEP 5: If you know the age of the person at death, add appropriate signs of aging and hairstyle.

CHECK THIS OUT!
IT'S FROM MY FORENSICS CLASS.

Pictures of the final work in our example ran in a newspaper in 1989. Someone recognized the once-unknown face as Karen Price—and later, two men were charged with her murder.

June 2, 2007

LOOK IN THE MIRROR TO SEE IF THIS INFO IS TRUE ABOUT YOU!

TIPS FOR SHAPING THE FACE

- The inner borders of the iris in a person's eyes are directly over the corners of the mouth.
- The distance between the inner corners of the eyes is about the same as the width of the nose.
- The nose and ears are about the same in length (but older people have longer ears).

Trying to rebuild a face from just a skull can be like reconstructing a piece of fruit from an apple core. It's part art, part science, and part guesswork. Hopefully, when you're done, the face will look enough like the living person that an identification can be made.

I reconstruct faces with clay. To do this, I've had to learn tons about human anatomy. Like the depth of flesh on the average face—and the way the muscles, wrinkles, and fat can change someone's appearance. The trickiest parts are soft tissue areas like the eyes, nose, and mouth, where there aren't any bones to help guide you.

As I worked, I thanked my lucky stars that this skull was a replica. I wouldn't have to use maggots to clean the flesh from the skull before starting work (like one of my professors made us do!). These bugs chow down the remaining tissue on a skull and leave it sparkling clean—but a maggot is the one thing that can gross me out!

Some people I know use computer tomography (CT) scans instead of clay to build a face. The computer does lots of the work for you by laying down different faces over a picture of the skull until it come across one that looks right. It's not as messy and won't damage a skull. But the programmer still has to guess which faces to use and how to form soft tissue areas, so I stick with clay—

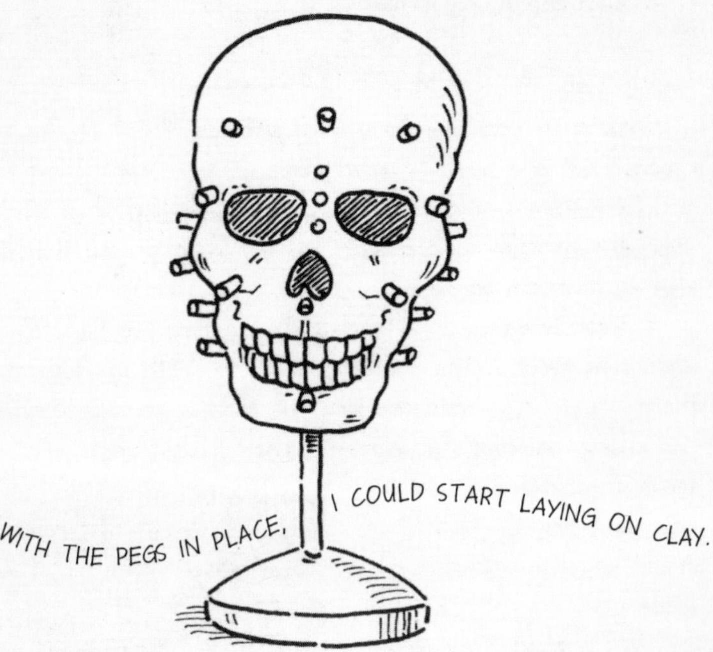

WITH THE PEGS IN PLACE, I COULD START LAYING ON CLAY.

Click!

I froze at the sound. This "click" was something I had heard thousands of times since I moved into this house. It was the sound of the front door closing. But very softly. As if someone were trying to stay undetected.

I realized with a jolt that I had forgotten to relock the front door. Anyone could have walked in—including the strange guy who shouted gibberish and threw the human skull at me.

The silence of the house filled my ears until it was almost unbearably loud.

I was just starting to think that I had imagined the click when I heard a very quiet scuffle, like the soles of someone's shoes rubbing against the marble of the front hall.

There was definitely someone in the house.

Silently rubbing the clay off my hands, I thought about calling out to see if it was Dad . . . but why would he be sneaking around? I glanced at the videophone. It was at the far side of the office away from the door.

If I darted for the phone, I'd be cornered up against the old garage door. I wouldn't be able to escape if someone came into the office.

Better to sprint out of the office and try to make it to the kitchen phone. There was a backdoor in the kitchen, so I wouldn't be trapped. Taking a deep breath, I bolted through the office door and sprinted toward the kitchen.

Heavy footsteps pounded down the hall behind me. I was being chased! Suddenly I felt my legs being swept out from under me. It was an expert move—but I managed to stick out my hand and catch myself on the wall. I kept my balance.

But it was clear I wasn't going to get away from the intruder. It was time to put some of Judge's training to work. I executed a quick turn and took a defensive stance.

And found Maura, the pilot, looking at me with that same stony expression.

"Hey!" I shouted. "What are you doing creeping around my house?"

"You left the front door open."

I felt myself flush. She was right. I had made a stupid mistake, especially since I had just come back from three weeks of detective training. "What? Do you go around tripping everyone who leaves a door open?" I demanded.

She calmly crossed her arms. "Judge Pinkerton told me to return and said that there might be trouble. I wasn't sure

MAURA PLANNED TO "TAKE CHARGE"!

who you were or if you might be armed. I'm here to take charge of the situation."

"If by 'take charge' you mean 'stay out of my way so I can find my dad,' then sure, I guess that would work."

"Whatever you say," she said coolly.

"Come on," I retorted. "I have to get back to work."

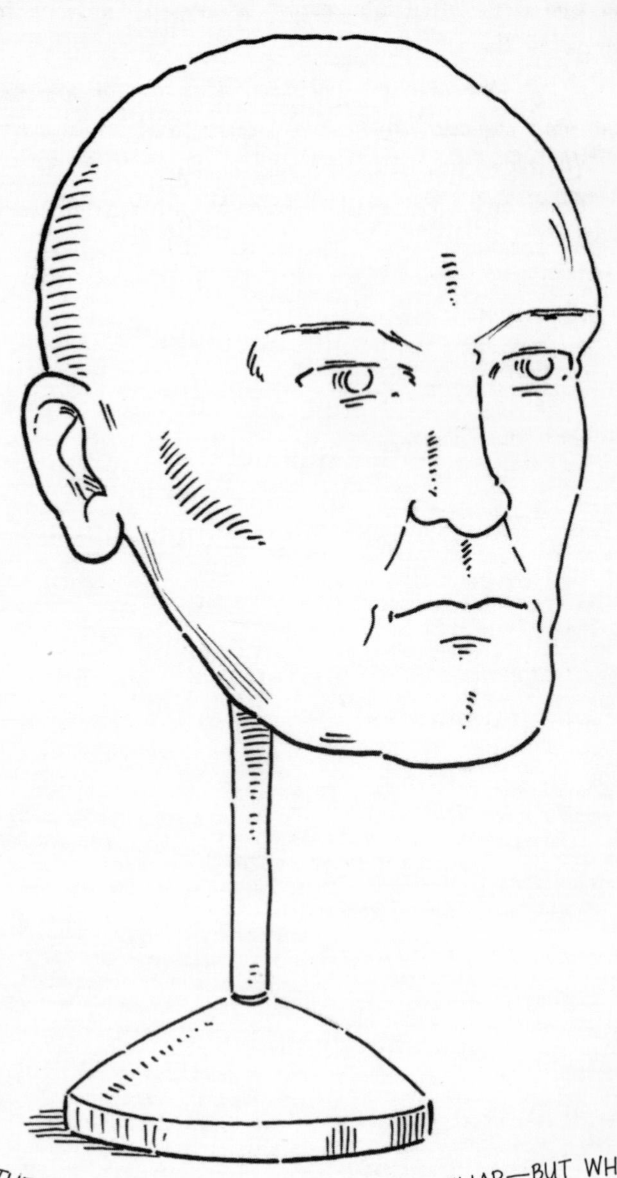

THE RECONSTRUCTED FACE LOOKED FAMILIAR—BUT WHY?

June 2, 2007

7:30 PM

For the next three hours, I worked on reconstructing the face over the skull. Maura had made a sweep through the house—checking to make sure that there were no intruders or a ransom note that I had missed. But, like me, she had come up empty-handed. There were no concrete clues as to what had happened to my dad.

Now she was perched on the edge of Dad's desk, watching me work. "I think you might be wasting your time. Your dad's probably just at the store or the movies," Maura said. "He wasn't expecting you to be home for another week. Maybe he went out of town."

"I hope so," I said, gently pushing a piece of clay onto the skull. "But Judge spoke with him this morning. She told him I'd be home today."

Finally, the head was done. I took a step back and looked at my work: It was a man. And he had a face that looked familiar to me.

"Does this look like anyone you know?" I asked Maura. "Or knew?"

She stood and moved closer to examine the head. "I can't put my finger on it," Maura said thoughtfully, "but his face is ringing a bell."

I nodded in agreement. Bells were definitely ringing. But who was he?

I grabbed my digital camera, snapped a quick pic, and downloaded it to my computer.

"What are you doing?" Maura asked.

June 2, 2007

"My dad got us this cool facial recognition software," I told her. "You just put in a photograph of someone's face. The program looks at skin texture and facial characteristics, like the distance between the eye sockets or the point of a nose. Then it tries to match the face you put in to others in the database. It's not as good as a fingerprint. But since the skull is all we have to work with . . ."

"I didn't think there was a central database with everyone's faces," Maura observed.

"There isn't," I agreed. "So I just told my computer to check with the different databases around the world that do—including those in museums. It's going to take a while to go through all those photos."

JUST THE FACTS

In the early 1990s, researchers developed EIGENFACES, a facial recognition program that zeroes in on 128 different points on a person's face (from photos, video, or sketches). It compares those points to other people's faces and looks for a match.

The United States Marshals Service recently used the Illinois facial reconstruction database to track down info on one of their 15 Most Wanted fugitives. After entering the booking photo of Daniel Escobedo, the system scanned over eight million driver's license images in the database. The man's license popped up first within seconds.

I USE A VERSION OF THIS SOFTWARE

June 2, 2007

With my computer working away, I examined the face again. "How do I know you?" I asked it.

In a flash, something popped into my head. "My dad always says, 'Nick, you can tell a lot about a person by where they look when you're talking to them.'"

Maura looked at her watch, as if she wasn't sure how long she'd have to be here. "That's a nice saying." Her tone was one you would use with a little kid.

"How about the mystery man?" I wondered out loud. "Where is he looking?"

I grabbed a tape measure. I hooked one end to the top of the face and extended the tape, following the face's gaze across the room as if it were a straight arrow. The face's line of "vision" traveled over the mess on the floor to the bookshelf.

June 2, 2007

On a whim, I removed one of the books from the general area in which the skull was looking. It was a book about trains in 1906. I flipped quickly through the pages and then gave the book a shake. No secret note fell out. I took another book down from the same area and got the same results. Nothing.

I was just turning away from the bookshelf, when something caught my eye.

BAM!

The polished metal corner of some kind of door shone through the space I had made in the bookshelf. There was something hidden behind the other volumes. Maura noticed it, too. Together, we removed the rest of the books from that shelf.

Soon we were looking at the door of a hidden safe.

My heartbeat kicked up a notch.

"You didn't know this safe was back there?" Maura asked.

I shook my head. "Dad must have known that I would put the skull in the same place I always do—and that when I reconstructed the face, it would be looking at this spot!"

I yanked on the safe door, but it wouldn't budge. It was locked tight. I looked more closely—the safe had a small microphone.

SPY SHOP

Congratulations on your purchase of the Sez-U 2200 Safe! Key locks have been replaced by biometrics. The safe will only open for people with authorized "voiceprints" and the correct password. Why is this better? You can forget your keys—but you can't forget your voice!

THIS IS THE SAFE MY DAD BOUGHT

Oh, no, I thought. That meant it had a voice recognition lock.

There were tons of biometric systems in our house—like the locks on the doors, the lights, and even the TV remote. The systems were able to read different human characteristics, like the shape of the face, fingerprints, and voice patterns. For example, if you didn't have the right retina, the front door wouldn't unlock for you.

"My dad set all the biometrics systems in the house to accept voice commands from him and me," I told Maura. "But this safe is different. To open it, you not only need the right voice—which I have—but also the correct password—which I don't have."

Maura tapped a finger against her lips, clearly trying to think of a way into the safe. I was glad she didn't suggest that I just "safecrack" it.

TALK ABOUT WORKING UNDER PRESSURE...

Safecracking Down Under

In the early twentieth century, Charles Courtney had two loves: mechanical things (especially locks) and undersea diving. He decided to combine his two loves and went to work as a safecracker on sunken ships. The first person to crack a safe 400 feet underwater, he recovered millions of dollars during his career!

Thanks to Hollywood, lots of people think it's easy for a detective or a safecracker to unlock a safe. But most safecrackers don't use stethoscopes to listen to clicking lock tumblers like in the movies. That would take much too long and might not even lead to success. Instead, they drill through the casing, smash the safe open, or just blow the door off.

I didn't have the equipment for any of that. I started trying passwords. "Unlock," I said. The safe made a harsh BUZZ! sound and stayed locked. I had guessed wrong.

Hmmm . . . any good investigator knows that most people use their birthdays or names of relatives as passwords. I tried my dad's birthday and then my own, and the safe buzzed twice. I spoke my name "Nick"—BUZZ!—and my dad's "Henry"—BUZZ!

Maura calmly raised an eyebrow, as if to say, What are you doing?

For some reason, her calm only frustrated me more and I yelled, "I don't know!"

BUZZ!

Suddenly, a woman's pleasant voice came from the safe. "Due to six unsuccessful password attempts, security measure 865 is now in place. If you fail twice more, the contents of the safe will be destroyed to protect them from wrongful possession."

I forced my mouth closed. I had been about to make another guess at the password—but now every guess counted.

I ONLY HAD TWO MORE CHANCES
TO FIGURE OUT THE PASSWORD!

I gestured for Maura to follow me away from the safe, so that it wouldn't overhear our conversation and think that we were trying out passwords.

"I need you to help me brainstorm," I said to her when we were huddled in the corner.

"Okay," she said, her eyes focused intently on me. "You've tried all the types of words I would have tried. I have the feeling that it is something only you would know. Has your father said anything to you lately that was only between the two of you?"

My mind started working. Dad and I shared a lot of stuff, but I couldn't think of anything that could be boiled down into a password. I shook my head.

But Maura wasn't giving up. "So he hasn't said anything to you lately that struck you as a little strange?"

"No," I answered. "But someone else has."

I reminded Maura that the strange guy at the door had uttered some kind of nutty phrase before running off.

"Could that be it?" Maura looked doubtful.

"The skull that the man gave me led us to the safe, so maybe what he said will open it." Without waiting for her to respond, I rushed across the room. "Wonefas nepo!" I shouted.

There wasn't even time for me to get my hopes up—BUZZ!

We had one more chance. Slow down, Nick, and think! I told myself.

I entered the words "Wonefas nepo" into my universal translator on my handheld PC, and it came up with nothing. Was I on the wrong track? Did I have the whole thing backward?

That's it! I had the whole phrase backward!

I reversed the order of the phrase, letter for letter, and spoke with confidence: "Open safe now!"

There was a soothing BING! and the door to the safe popped open.

THERE WAS A MESSAGE IN THE SAFE!

June 2, 2007

9:30 PM

For a second, I wondered why my dad hadn't created a more complicated code to open the safe—like something he might have learned from my Uncle Zeke. Then the answer came to me: My dad couldn't make the code too tricky or I might not have been able to crack it.

But I had!

I mentally patted myself on the back and reached eagerly into the safe, pulling out a scrap of paper. It was the only thing in the safe, and it had a message written in my dad's handwriting.

I showed the note to Maura. Now that we had the safe open, it was okay to talk in a normal voice.

"The words are obvious," I said. "Dad is congratulating me on getting into the safe."

"But what about the numbers?" Maura wondered. "What do they mean?"

"Are they a date like 12/25?" I mused. "Is he talking about Christmas?"

Maura offered, "Maybe it's a chapter and verse of something. . . ."

I shook my head. None of the stuff we were guessing sounded right.

"Could it be a time?"

I quickly scanned the office, searching for a clock. I didn't see one anywhere. But I did notice something else about the room. I slapped my forehead in frustration.

"What?" Maura asked.

"I should have seen this ages ago!" I handed her the photo I'd taken of the office a few hours ago.

"I still don't see it. . . ." Her eyes went wide as she understood. "Oh! Of course!"

I climbed up on a chair and looked down at the mess on the office floor. This time I really studied it. Yes, I was right. It was not just a random group of objects.

I said, "The mess was very deliberately laid out in the shape of a clock!"

REMEMBERING THESE SKETCHES
HELPED ME SEE THE CLOCK IN THE MESS.

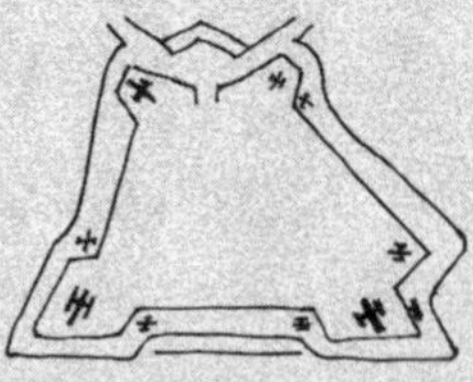

Founder of the Boy Scout movement, **Robert Baden-Powell** (1857–1941), sketched a moth on a twig while along the coast of the Adriatic Sea. Baden-Powell was actually an English spy, and his drawing of a moth concealed the plan of an enemy fortress.

I grabbed a yardstick for the minute hand and a large book for the hour hand. I placed them on the shape of the clock face on the floor, so that the time read 12:25.

I wondered, "Does this mean he was kidnapped at 12:25?"

Maura shook her head. "How would he have time to set up a clock if he was being kidnapped?"

"You're right," I agreed. "Maybe the words on his note aren't as obvious as I thought."

I took another look at the note. I reread the line "Give yourself a big hand!"

"A big hand . . . big hand . . . BIG HAND! That's it!" I cried. "My dad is talking about the big hand of the clock. He wants me to go where the big hand is pointing."

I followed its direction to a poster that leaned against the wall. It was a picture of Mount Everest.

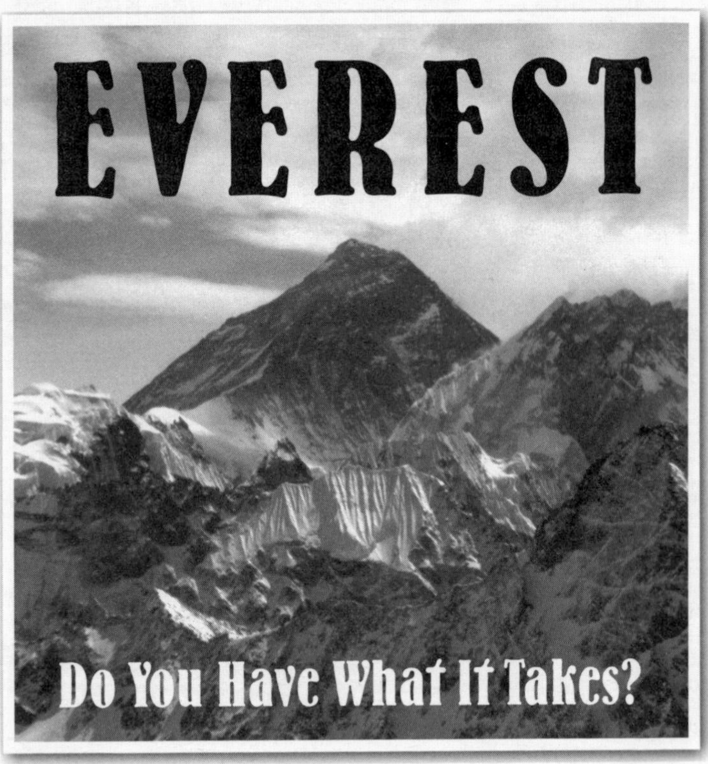

Just as I was reaching for the poster, my computer chimed, telling me it had identified the face I had reconstructed.

Maura and I rushed over and looked at the screen. One name flashed there: GEORGE MALLORY.

"George Mallory?" Maura asked. "The mountain climber?"

"That's the only George Mallory I know."

It was very strange. Mallory had died on Mount Everest more than 80 years ago. He had hoped to be the first person to ever climb the world's highest mountain. And he may have succeeded. The only thing people know is that Mallory died at some point during the climb. No one is sure if it was before or after he made it to the top.

The man who got credit for being the first to person to summit Mount Everest is Sir Edmund Hillary. And he made his successful climb in 1953, nearly thirty years after Mallory died on the mountain.

It was one of the biggest mysteries in the past hundred years. Did Mallory make it to the top of Everest or not? Was he actually the first one there—and not Hillary?

An even bigger mystery in my mind was: Why did someone throw a replica of Mallory's skull in my hands and then run off?

Maura and I stared at the flashing name on my screen for a moment longer. Then I went back to the poster of Mount Everest.

"Let's get a better look at this under the desk light," I said, lifting the poster up away from the wall. As I was placing it on the desk, my fingers brushed against something on the back.

I flipped the poster over and carefully set it facedown on the desk. There was a large envelope taped to the back.

24 STILL TO SOLVE MAGAZINE

MOUNTAIN MYSTERY?

by R. S. Grafton

Born in England in 1886, George Mallory was an expert mountaineer who wanted to be the first to climb to the top of Mount Everest. In 1924, after two unsuccessful attempts, Mallory tried for the third time. As he neared the top, he was caught in bad weather and disappeared. His body wasn't discovered until 1999. Did Mallory die before or after he reached the top? No one knows. Perhaps he was the first person to summit Everest, but no proof has ever been found. In 1953, Sir Edmund Hillary officially became the first person to reach the top.

"And the clues keep on coming," I said under my breath. I slowly pulled the envelope free and opened it.

Inside was a piece of paper. Maura looked over my shoulder as I held it under the desk light to get a better look.

"That's a copy of a page from a climbing diary," Maura said.

"And look," I added, pointing to the name on the page. "The diary belonged to George Mallory. It's a list of the things he took with him on an expedition."

I told her about the screenplay my dad was writing, and how it was about explorers from the past. "My dad likes to really feel the objects as he writes about them," I told her. "He says it helps with his descriptions. So he gathers together the stuff he needs."

We went to the side of my dad's desk, and I showed Maura the large cardboard box where he'd been storing stuff for his script. Maura read the items on the list and checked them off when I found them in the box.

"Gloves," she called out.

I dug around for a second and found them. "Check."

"Oxygen tank."

More rooting around and I plucked out the tank. "Check."

Everything was in the box until Maura came to the last item on the list. "Kodak Vest Pocket camera," she read aloud.

I did some more digging in the box, but this time I came up empty-handed. The camera wasn't there.

The camera!

Suddenly, the lyrics in that goofy song my dad had recorded on the MP3 player made sense. I told Maura how my dad used the words "shutter," "bug," and "develop" in his song.

"Everything has been leading up to that," I said, thinking out loud. "The key must lie with the camera."

Maura looked doubtful. "The camera shouldn't be here, Nick. It was never found."

"That's right!" I agreed. "It was lost somewhere toward the top of Mount Everest. If Mallory climbed to the summit, he might have taken a picture of himself there. In other words, the film in the camera might show whether Mallory was the first person to make it to the top of Everest. It could solve the Mallory mystery once and for all."

SHUTTERBUG MAGAZINE

THE VEST POCKET MODEL B was introduced by **Kodak** in 1924. This pocket-sized folding camera may have looked just like larger folding cameras—except for its size and that it used little rolls of film that could make tiny 1 5/8–inch by 2 1/2–inch exposures. The original Vest Pocket Camera was popular with soldiers during World War I and cost about six dollars. The Model B had a new "autographic" feature that allowed users to slide open a little window and write information like the time and date through backing paper directly onto the film.

As I spoke, I realized what I'd have to do to find my dad. But how would I ever reach my destination, which was halfway around the world?

Aha! I looked at Maura.

She held up a hand. "I know what you're going to say. And it's crazy."

"You were here when we put the clues together. I think my dad has been kidnapped because of that camera, and I think he's telling me that he's with the camera or heading toward it. He left the clues because he wants me to come and help him." I could see that Maura wasn't buying this. Trying to sound as commanding as possible, I said, "Judge Pinkerton told you to take me to my father."

"Yes, she did, Nick," she replied with a cocked eyebrow. "But I don't think she ever dreamed that meant taking you to another hemisphere. Do you?"

I shrugged. "Let's call her and see what she says."

"You and I both know that's she going to be out of touch for the next few days," Maura said. "But I'll give it a shot."

I watched as she tried a series of different numbers on her cell phone. Finally, she snapped it shut. "I can't get through to any of her numbers."

"You really don't need to," I said. "I'm telling you, Judge would want you to take me to my dad."

Maura was shaking her head. Still no sale. "What about a family member or friend you can trust?" she asked.

I thought about my godfather, Benny, and about my cousin, Helen Moorie. Could they help me? But then I quickly dismissed those options.

"Why didn't my dad call anyone else for help?" I asked. "There must be a reason why he left such a complicated series of clues that only I could follow. It's clear that my dad wanted me to piece them together on my own."

With Maura's face still stony, I decided to try a different approach to getting what I wanted. I said, "'To refuse the adventure is to run the risk of drying up like a pea in its shell.'"

Rolling her eyes, Maura asked, "And what does that have to do with anything?"

"It's something that George Mallory once said."

"You know, I think you're confusing adventure with madness," Maura proclaimed. Clearly, quoting famous people wasn't going to convince her, either.

"Look," I said, "Judge told you not to trust the police just now. Right?"

Reluctantly, Maura nodded. "That's true . . . " Something in her eyes softened.

"So who else can I turn to?" I asked. "You have a plane, I have my passport . . . "

Once again, she shook her head. "Let's just wait—"

"But while we're waiting, my dad could be in danger!" I exclaimed.

GEORGE MALLORY

"But you're asking me to fly you out of the country. . . ." Maura's eyes looked away for a moment. "I'd have to file a flight plan—No!

This is crazy! We're not even sure where your dad is."

She had snapped back from it, but she'd begun talking about the trip as if it were a real possibility. I would have to somehow seal the deal. I remembered something Judge had said to me as I was leaving PDA. "Judge told me we have something in common," I said. "What is it?"

Maura just looked at me. "I don't know what she meant."

Inspiration struck. "Did something happen to your parents, too?" I asked. "Like with my biological parents?"

Pain flashed across her face, and I could see that I had struck a nerve. Suddenly, I felt really guilty. I didn't want to use something painful to get my way. "I'm sorry," I said quietly and backed off.

MAURA FINALLY GAVE IN!

I didn't say anything else. Sometimes the best thing you can do as a detective is just shut your mouth.

Maura's lips were set in a firm line. She stared back at me. "Drying up like a pea in its shell, huh?" she said, almost to herself.

A few more moments passed in silence.

Finally, Maura threw up her hands. "But the camera is on Mount Everest!" she shouted.

I smiled. I knew she was in.

"Then you'd better pack a winter coat," I said.

IN MY DREAM, JUDGE WARNED ME ABOUT TRUSTING PEOPLE.

June 5, 2007

2:15 AM

"You have to be careful, Nick," Judge whispered. She was leaning on her driftwood cane, and we were standing near the door in her darkened office at PDA. Moonlight slanted through the window blinds and a lamp on her desk cast an eerie circle of light.

I had the sinking feeling that something awful was about to happen . . . or had already happened.

But I was so happy to see Judge. "We've been trying to reach you," I told her. For some reason I was whispering, too. "Is everything okay?"

Judge glanced over my shoulder. Smiling, she put a hand on my arm and tried to soothe me. "You'll be fine, as long as you follow my advice."

My head was spinning and I couldn't remember what she had told me.

"Relax, Nick," she said gently. "I just advised you to be careful about whom you trust."

"Okay—"

"Especially that person." Judge's blue eyes flicked once again to the space behind me. I turned to follow her gaze. There was nothing but an open door and beyond that . . . darkness.

I glanced back to ask Judge what she meant—but she was gone!

"Judge?" I whispered, my stomach clenching in panic. The office was empty. Judge had vanished.

A scratching noise brought my attention back to the doorway.

June 5, 2007

A dark, menacing figure was detaching itself from the shadows outside. I couldn't make out who it was—but he or she seemed familiar somehow. The figure was coming through the door. And just from the way it moved, I knew that I was in danger.

Terror struck me, but I forced myself to remain still. I needed to see the identity of the person that Judge was warning me about.

Hands emerged from the darkness and before I could turn to run—they were suddenly shaking me.

I woke up from the dream with a start. I found myself looking into Maura's icy green eyes.

"You were having a nightmare, Nick," she said matter-of-factly, removing her hand from my shoulder. "I thought it best to wake you up."

The shadows of the dream slipped away. In a flash, I remembered that I was sitting in the co-pilot's seat of the Learjet. I rubbed drool from the side of my mouth. Maura, who sat in the pilot's seat, turned back to the controls of the plane. They were a dizzying array of blinking lights, spinning dials, and electronic readouts. If the controls were this complicated on a small jet, I wondered what they must look like on a 747.

But the blinking lights didn't hold my interest for long. I was too busy looking at Maura.

Dad always said I should follow my instincts. Had the dream been my subconscious telling me to beware? Was Maura someone who shouldn't be trusted?

As if sensing my inner struggle, Maura turned again and cocked an eyebrow at me. "What's up?"

"Nothing," I replied, pushing aside my growing suspicions. This was silly. Maura wasn't the bad guy. "I guess I'm just tired," I told her. "Traveling for two days will do that. Any luck reaching Judge Pinkerton while I slept?"

Maura shook her head. "No, and I've been trying constantly."

Disappointed, I asked, "Where are we now?"

"Over the Khumbu Valley in Nepal," she answered. "We're approaching the airstrip in the village of Lukla."

THE HIMALAYAS WERE AMAZING!

I was glad Maura had woken me up. The views outside the window were spectacular. Beneath a sky more blue than I ever imagined, the Himalayas spread out like giant, natural sky-scrapers made of rock, ice, and snow. Because they were so high above sea level, the peaks of the mountains were shrouded in drifting white clouds.

Two days ago, we had flown from Los Angeles to Kathmandu. There we spent a day wrangling permission from

Nepal's government to fly into the mountains. Now we were approaching Lukla. The small village had the closest airstrip to Mount Everest that could accommodate the landing of a Learjet.

Below us, the Khumbu Valley spread out in all its splendor. Green fields bordered by glistening streams gave way to the gray rocks of the mountains. The valley was the gateway to the southern approach to Mount Everest.

Maura and I had discussed earlier that in 1953 when Sir Edmund Hillary made the trip from Kathmandu to Lukla, it had taken him three weeks. According to the Nepali guidebook I had printed from the Internet before we left, Hillary had had to travel on foot and deal with five-inch-long bloodsucking leeches dropping from the trees. The trip by plane was only two hours.

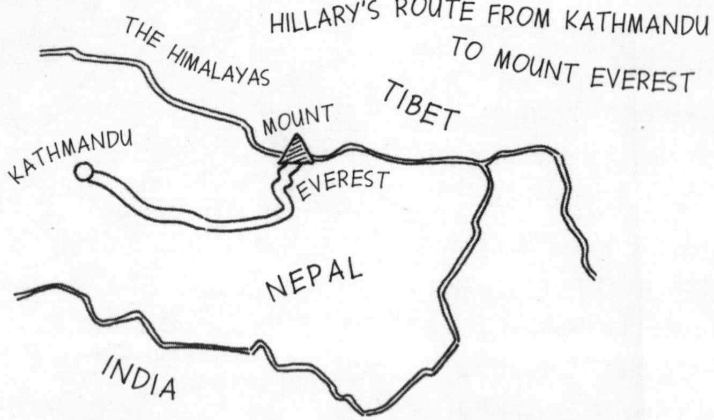

"Prepare for landing," Maura said, breaking into my thoughts.

"What?" I asked, startled. I was still looking out the window. All I saw were mountains and more mountains. "Where are you going to land?"

"The airstrip." She pointed down.

THE LUKLA AIRSTRIP IS REALLY SHORT!

I squinted and finally spotted a sliver of pavement perched precariously on the side of a mountain. A tiny village, which must be Lukla, butted up against the strip.

I think someone forgot to tell whoever built the strip that planes, not gnats, were going to land here.

As we descended, I could see a group of villagers gathered halfway up the mountain. They were pointing at us, clearly watching our approach—almost as if they expected us to crash.

Looking back at the impossibly small airstrip, I expected the same thing.

"This is crazy!" I shouted.

But Maura remained calm. The corners of her mouth twitched. "I bet those bloodsucking leeches are sounding pretty good right now," she said, the closest thing to a joke I'd ever heard her say.

June 5, 2007

I couldn't laugh. The nightmare I'd had earlier was nothing compared to the terror of this!

The plane went almost completely vertical for a moment, and I was looking straight down. Swirling air created by the nearby mountains slammed into us. My head bumped up against the ceiling. I pulled the strap of my seat belt more tightly around me and held on.

Maura leveled out the plane at the last second. I was impressed not only with myself for keeping my eyes open the entire time, but also with Maura for the way she managed to bring the plane down safely and relatively smoothly.

"Wow," was all I could manage to say as the plane came to a halt near a small building that I guess served as the terminal.

We unbuckled our seat belts and climbed out of the plane. Maura looked as relaxed as if she made this kind of landing every day, but my feet had never been happier to be on solid ground. The air was crisp and pure and was a pleasant 60 degrees or so. At this altitude, I knew the oxygen levels in the air would be much lower than I was used to.

Some people can develop altitude sickness or hypoxia. This sickness can get really bad. In fact, it can lead to hallucinations and messed-up decisions. Thanks to the last three weeks of training in the mountains around PDA, I thought I had a head start on getting acclimated, or used to, the higher altitudes.

Maura said we should wait by the plane. A tall, dark-haired man wearing a gray business suit was already walking across the tarmac toward us. Two armed soldiers strode behind him.

"That must be the government official. Give me your passport and let me handle this," Maura said quietly to me.

OUR GREETERS AT THE AIRSTRIP

"No problem," I replied, happy to avoid dealing with the gun-toting soldiers. "I'll get our bags and wait for you over by the terminal."

I grabbed our two backpacks and made my way over to the small building. My head had started buzzing, and I felt the twinges of nausea in my gut.

Telling myself to stop being such a baby, I watched as Maura shook hands with the dark-haired man. She handed him our passports. I heard a few words, including Judge Pinkerton's name. At the mention of her, the man smiled and the soldiers backed off slightly. Obviously, even here, Judge's name carries some weight.

Then the wind picked up, and I couldn't hear anything else.

Luckily, I can read lips.

I saw the dark-haired man say the words: "A private plane landed here yesterday."

Maura glanced over at me quickly and then turned away. She indicated that the man should do so as well. They both had their backs to me, and I couldn't hear or see any more of their conversation.

After a moment, Maura and the man shook hands. I saw her tell him that we would be back for the plane within a week. The man smiled, and I could see him say, "No problem. No problem."

The man told the soldiers they could go, and Maura led the man over toward me. He asked if I was bringing any food or dangerous substances into the village. When I answered no, he handed our passports back to us and told us to have a nice day.

I saw him give Maura a look. A silent communication seemed to pass between them.

Or was I just imagining things?

My head was really starting to pound now. Maura and I slung our packs over our shoulders and headed through the terminal. I was bursting with questions. Had the official seen my dad? Had he been on the plane that landed yesterday? But Maura held a finger to her lips and said, "Let's wait to talk."

We made our way into the village, which cascaded down the side of the mountain at seemingly impossible angles. The hard-packed dirt road twisted and turned through the various one-story buildings. The window frames and doorframes of the wood houses, inns, and businesses were painted in cobalt blue or other bright colors. Villagers bustled about, some carrying goods to trade, others shopping. There were women with bright purple and red shawls wrapped loosely around their heads and some of the men wore "dokos," a kind of backpack. The tourists were easy to spot—because of the way they were dressed and the cameras most of them had slung around their necks.

LUKLA VILLAGERS

But the buzzing in my head was growing louder. And I was having a tough time concentrating on anything, let alone the pleasant postcard setting.

"You have to tell me," I demanded impatiently. "Did you ask that man if he'd seen my dad?"

Maura stopped walking, seeming surprised by my urgency. "The official told me that no other private planes have landed here in the last day."

"What?" I stammered. That isn't what he had said . . . or maybe I had misread his lips. "Are you sure?"

"I was standing right next to him. So, yes, I'm sure."

The involuntary twitch of the corners of her eyes and the quick jerking movement in her shoulders told me all I needed to know.

She was lying!

I was too stunned to speak. Had my dream been an accurate warning after all? Had I just flown to a distant country with someone whom it was dangerous to trust? But why would Judge have sent Maura to help me if she wasn't trustworthy? Had Maura actually managed to fool her?

June 5, 2007

If only my head would stop ringing, maybe I could piece it all together. But I couldn't seem to catch my breath. . . .

"Can I see your guidebook?" Maura asked, apparently oblivious to my inner doubts. Without a word, I handed her the book. She flipped to the map and studied it for a second. Then she looked at me. "You seem tired. Should we bunk here in the village tonight?"

"No," I said absently. "Our plan is to catch up to my dad before he reaches Mount Everest. And we won't do that if we go to sleep."

"Okay. You're right. There's still plenty of daylight. I think we can make our way to Phakding. We'll be that much closer to Everest the next day."

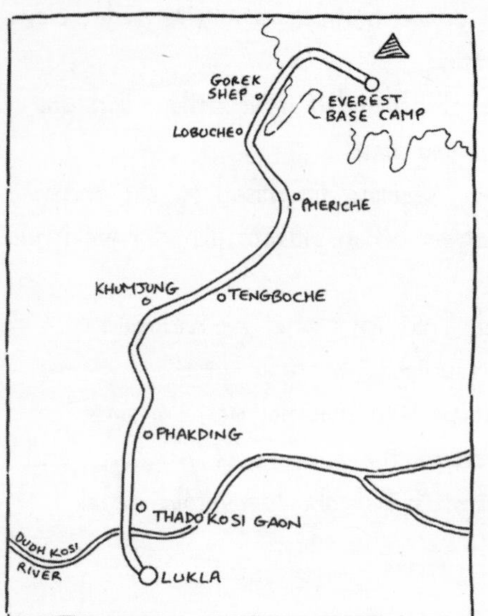

Maura and I headed west, and the road took us out of the village and soon became a wide dirt path, which dropped steeply. Then the trail turned north and descended once again to a village called Thado Kosi Gaon. We hiked through an enormous green field. I was surprised by all the tall grass and yellow wildflowers. I always imagined the area around Everest would be rocky and snow-covered.

My head now felt like it had been stuffed with a pillow full of angry bees. But I was able to come to a decision:

I would pretend that everything was fine between Maura and me until I had a chance to act.

We crossed over the Dudh Kosi river on a rickety wood bridge and twenty minutes later, we reached Phakding. The sun was going down as we entered the small village. Two men walked by, leading a large yak.

SO YOU WANT TO BUY A YAK?

Check out our handy guide below and find out why you should go mild—not wild!

	WILD YAKS	DOMESTIC YAKS
Maximum height at shoulder	**6.5 feet**	**5.5 feet**
Maximum weight	**1,800 pounds**	**900 pounds**
Maximum length of horns	**3 feet**	**Varies, sometimes none**

Yaks are found primarily in Nepal and China at altitudes of about 6,500 to 16,000 feet, where temperatures can drop to 40 degrees below zero. These surefooted animals can travel narrow, rocky trails and wade through deep snow while packing heavy loads. Yaks also provide wool for clothing and leather for shoes, as well as milk, butter, and cheese. Their manure is used to fertilize fields and as fuel in treeless areas. Today, due to hunting (now illegal), there are only about 15,000 wild yaks. Domestic yaks number about 14 million. So go mild—not wild!

Now's my chance, I thought.

I acted as if I'd stumbled on a loose rock on the road. I fell against the yak. It smelled horrible! With my hand hidden from view, I quickly plucked several hairs out of the beast.

The yak was enormous—but apparently pretty sensitive. It let out a little grunt of pain. One of the men yelled something in Nepali at me, but they kept walking.

"What just happened?" Maura asked.

"Nothing." If Maura was going to keep secrets, than I decided I had better do so, as well. I tucked the yak hairs into my pocket for safekeeping.

We continued on our way through the tiny village, which was really just a group of small houses and businesses. The blue- and green-painted roofs reminded me of the wildflowers we'd passed on our trek. Thankfully, most of the signs in the village were written in Nepali and English, so we could read the one for the Mountain Inn and Lodging. It was a two-story stone building, which had been painted a dark pink.

Inside the tiny lobby of the inn, there were several groups of other Americans here for the night. Each group was being led by one or two muscular men with smooth brown skin. These must be Sherpas, I thought.

I walked up to several of the travelers and Sherpas. I showed them a photo of my dad I had taken last New Year's Eve. His short dark hair framed his good-looking face. And he was giving his trademark toothy grin.

Unfortunately, no one in the lobby, including the young receptionist behind the counter, had seen my dad. But he did say that the inn had two available rooms for the night. He also told us that dinner

ABOUT THE SHERPAS

The first Sherpas migrated from Tibet to Nepal about 500 years ago. Now there are roughly 10,000 Sherpas in Nepal, about 3,000 of them in the Khumbu valley. Their skills and physical strength at high altitudes are unmatched, and Sherpas are usually a vital part of any successful climbing expedition. Before climbing became such a major industry, most Sherpas were traders.

was now being served in the dining room.

Just the word "dinner" was enough to make my mouth water. Rather than dropping our bags in our rooms, Maura and I headed straight to the chow.

The lodge's simple dining room had a long wooden table and equally long benches on either side. We sat with other travelers. My detective's ears picked up Australian and German accents. Down the table, four people from Japan were celebrating a successful climb up Mount Everest. Maura and I ate in silence.

We ordered a traditional Sherpa stew, "shyakpa," a meat-and-potatoes dish with vegetables. Normally, I would have loved the spicy beef and vegetable stew, but my stomach was feeling as bad as my head. After we ate, we headed up the stairs to the second floor and our rooms.

As I was unlocking my door, Maura asked me, "Are you sure you're okay, Nick? Do you want me to get a doctor?"

What was she talking about? Was this some kind of trick? I felt fine!

But I just shook my head. "I guess I must look tired, that's all. It's been a long trip."

"Okay, then," she said. "If you're sure. Good night."

"'Night," I said.

We went into our separate rooms. Mine was a simple room, with just a bed, a chair, a lamp, and a window that overlooked the dark street.

I told myself it didn't matter what the room was like. I wouldn't be staying there.

I gave myself a second to look at the bed longingly. My eyes were burning, I was so tired, and that strange ringing in my ears was now deafening.

But I had work to do. And sleeping wouldn't help me find my dad.

I unzipped my backpack and removed the slide with a long hair on it. This was the hair that was stuck to the piece of cloth that had torn off the strange man's coat back in Los Angeles.

I dug back into my pack and pulled out my compact microscope. I unfolded it and placed it on the bed. I compared the slide to one of the hairs I had plucked off the poor yak in the street.

It was just as I thought.

While the hairs weren't from the exact same animal (one of the hairs was much darker than the other), they had both come from the same type of creature. I had confirmed at least one thing. The hair I'd taken from the torn cloth had come from a yak. The analysis I'd done before leaving home was right.

So now that I was in the right area, I'd just have to find a yak farm to see if I could track down the strange man who had visited my house. And he might be able to lead me to my dad.

It all sounded like too much for me to deal with. . . .

I looked again at the bed. How great would it be to just curl up and go to sleep?

Or at the very least share my thoughts with Maura.

But Maura had lied to me about what the official had said at the airport. She couldn't be trusted.

There was a reason, I reminded myself, that Dad had left clues that only I could understand. I would have to head out on my own.

I looked at my pocket watch. It was almost two in the morning. There was no light coming through the window. Was I really prepared to wander off into the pitch-dark night on my own?

It was a gamble, but I didn't see any other choice. My dad was depending on me.

If I was going to do this, though, I had to disguise my appearance. Otherwise, someone like the receptionist might spot me leaving the inn and inform Maura.

June 5, 2007

STAR INTERVIEWS

"I was sick and tired of EVERYONE asking me for my autograph whenever I left the house, so I tried different disguises. The ones that work best are the simplest. I slick back my hair or mess it up. I walk differently or talk with an accent. I wear sunglasses or a hat. I never overdo the disguise—like with wigs or weird clothes—that would just draw attention to me."

— **Burt Garrett**, MOVIE STAR —

THIS ACTOR IS A FRIEND OF MY DAD'S.

IN THE MIRROR, I LOOKED LIKE SOMEONE ELSE.

After I packed up my microscope and my hair samples, I grabbed my thick down jacket and pulled the sleeves inside out, so it looked like I was wearing a different coat. Then, I turned my hat inside out so that it was gray instead of blue. These simple changes were enough to alter my appearance—or I least I think they were. For some reason, it's hard for me to stay focused now.

June 5, 2007

As I get ready to slip out the door and into the night, I realize my hands are trembling and my head is pounding.

I hope with all my heart this isn't the last journal entry I ever make.

I'm coming for you, Dad!

THE LAST BRIDGE BEFORE NAMCHE BAZAR

June 6, 2007

3:15 PM

Luckily, there was a full moon, and the rocky path was easy to spot. I set off from Phakding and followed the Dudh Kosi river south. Using a small flashlight from my backpack, I constantly checked my progress on the map.

I'd already gone a few hundred yards when I remembered that I should be going north. My fuzzy brain couldn't seem to get things straight. Back on the right track, I trekked along the west bank of the fast-moving river.

Hiking in the middle of the night in a strange, mountainous country is terrifying. Every time I heard a noise, I couldn't help imagining that wild creatures were eyeing me hungrily or that bandits were about to descend upon me.

I passed through the small village of Zamphuti, and the path climbed steeply. Now I was walking along a ridge high above the Dudh Kosi. One false step and I would plunge down into the churning waters. I crossed several swaying suspension bridges and passed through two more small towns that weren't even on my map. After crossing the river one last time, I trudged up a steep hill and finally spotted the much larger town of Namche Bazar.

Though it had been just a five-hour hike, it felt like a lifetime. But I had made it! I walked into Namche Bazar just as the sun was coming up over the mountains. I don't think I've ever been so happy to see a sunrise in my whole life. And as exhausted and out of it as I was, I still noticed that the view of Everest was breathtaking.

June 6, 2007

In the village streets, traders were already setting up their booths, preparing to sell pottery, cloth, and sweet-smelling meats. Tourists were emerging from several of the lodges, looking ready for a day of hiking or shopping. It was a great chance for me to find out if anyone had seen my dad. He would have had to pass through here if he was being taken to Everest. Maybe someone had seen him.

I showed his photo to several people but always got different variations of the same response. "No" or "Sorry, ol' chap" or just a shake of the head.

As I talked to different people, I started to feel my mind wander . . .

What's wrong with me? I wondered to myself. Must just be tired . . .

78 • THE ULTIMATE NEPAL GUIDE BOOK

Nepali is one of the languages spoken in Nepal.

Phrase Craze

Not sure which bus to take in Nepal?
Find the phrase you need—and more!—below.

ENGLISH	NEPALI
I	ma
My name is [your name]	mero naam [your name] ho
Yes or I have	chaa
No or I don't have	chhaina
Where	kata or kahan
Here	yaha
Good/pretty	ramro
Clean	safa
Dirty	phohar
Help!	guhaar!
Where does this bus go?	yo bus kahaa jaanchha?
How are you?	tapai lai kasto chha?
I don't feel well	malai sancho chhaina
I speak a little Nepali	ma ali nepali bolchhu

June 6, 2007

It was time to get to the real purpose of this visit. Time to track down the yak farmers.

I walked over to a Sherpa who was carrying a basket of potatoes across the small square. Using the vocabulary list in my guidebook, I asked him, "Can you point me in the direction of the yak farm, please?" in Nepali.

I heard someone laugh behind me.

When I turned, I discovered a short blonde woman wearing a pith helmet and a khaki jacket with lots of pockets. She looked as if she was going on safari. She was beaming at me. "Do you know that you are asking for a yak farm?" the woman said. She had an English accent.

THE ENGLISHWOMAN

"Yes," I said, a little put off by the fact that she was laughing at me. "I know it sounds strange, but I need to find a particular yak farm."

"How mysterious," the woman said. "I'm leading a tour of young people from London. But apparently, they've decided to sleep in. While I wait, it would be my pleasure to help you. Follow me."

The woman and I walked over to a nearby booth that was selling richly colored jackets. The woman spoke in rapid Nepali, and the trader responded. They were speaking too quickly for me to look up any words in my phrasebook.

June 6, 2007

THE TRADER

The woman translated for me. "The nice man says that there are two yak farms close by. Here, let me show you on your map."

I pulled out my map. And as I did, the hair sample and bit of cloth from my porch in Los Angeles fell to the ground. The trader picked it up and, before I could take it back, he was examining the cloth through the clear plastic bag. He turned to the Englishwoman and said something in Nepali.

The woman clapped her hands and smiled and nodded at the trader.

"What did he say?" I asked anxiously, taking back the cloth and hair sample.

"He says this cloth was made on a farm in Konar. I can show you where that is on your map." She pointed to a settlement a few miles away. "The hike will take about three or four hours."

I fumbled for the map as she handed it back to me. The Englishwoman asked me if I was sure I was okay. "You look a bit wonky, if you don't mind me saying."

I shook my head. "I'm fine," I told her. "Thank you for all your help." I looked down at my guidebook, thanked the trader in Nepali, and started off.

I made my way past Tengboche, home of a famous monastery. I was now 13,000 feet above sea level. The view of Mount Everest was even more spectacular from here. It towered over its mountain neighbors, Nuptse and Lohtse.

In just under three hours, I reached the yak farm the woman had pointed out to me on the map. It sat on the side of a gently sloping hill. A simple wire fence surrounded the property, where several dozen yaks grazed peacefully in the sun, their tails twitching lazily at flies every now and then.

THE MYSTERIOUS MAN FROM LOS ANGELES WAS HERE!

About a hundred feet away sat a two-story stone house. A man had just walked out the front door and held his hand up against the sunlight. He was looking away from me.

I quickly closed the distance between us before he could turn around.

"Hello?" I said when I was within a few feet of him.

He jumped slightly and whirled around. When he did, I almost couldn't believe my eyes. I had found him!

Here was the man who had tossed the skull at me in Los Angeles. He was wearing the same coat—I could see where he had torn it on the splinter—and he had the same birthmark under his right eye.

"You!" I shouted. Suddenly, I wasn't sure what I was going to do now that I had found him. My head was spinning, and everything seemed to be moving too fast.

The man eyed me suspiciously. He said something in Nepali. I consulted my guidebook and translated his words into, "Who are you?"

"You know me!" I told him fiercely. "You came to my house in America!"

He shook his head and said something else in Nepali.

It's one thing to detect that someone is lying when they are speaking English. But I wasn't sure if my liar radar would work properly when I couldn't understand what the person was saying! Especially since my head hurt so bad I thought it might explode.

I did know one thing. I wasn't leaving here until I got some answers.

"Where is my father?" I demanded. "What have you done with him?"

The man looked around and said something else. This time, his meaning was clear. He was inviting me inside.

"No way," I said.

The man held up a finger as if to say, "I'll be right back." He disappeared inside.

I snuck over to the door, but I couldn't hear sounds from inside. I went around to the side of the house and peered through a window. I was looking into the living room. It was neat and tidy with shiny wooden furniture. A table, a chair, and—

Maura.

She was in the living room, talking with the Sherpa.

I must have made a noise without realizing it, because suddenly, Maura looked over at the window. When she saw me peering through the glass, her face relaxed in genuine relief. She even smiled. Something I didn't think Maura would be able to fake.

She rushed out of the house and came around the corner before I could even think about running. She grabbed me by the shoulders. "Where did you go? Why did you run off on your own like that?"

Even more freckles had popped up around her face, and they made her look even prettier. She seemed to have let down her guard, and I could see the real person beneath her icy exterior.

MAURA WAS IN THE SHERPA'S HOUSE!

But this wasn't the right time for making new friends. The Sherpa had also left the house and stood next to us.

I took a step back and glared at them. "You two know each other? What have you done with my father?"

I moved toward the Sherpa. My body was stiffening and I felt my hands turning into fists. Maura stepped between us and pushed me back. I stumbled a few steps but managed to keep my balance.

"Stop it," Maura said and came toward me. "This man is one of your father's best friends."

"That's a lie!" I shot back.

Before I could wriggle away, Maura placed her hands on my shoulders and put her face close to mine. She spoke very slowly. "Nick, you're suffering from hypoxia. You've got altitude sickness. You're not thinking straight."

"That's crazy!" I cried.

"Is it?" Maura asked. "Think about the way you've been acting. You've got a huge headache, I bet, and feel really strange. And would anyone in his right mind do what you did last night? Sneak out of the inn in the pitch-dark? You could have fallen off a cliff! Not to mention you almost gave me a heart attack when I woke up this morning to find your room empty and your bed still made."

"You've been lying to me!" I shouted. "You're trying to stop me from finding my dad."

Maura shook her head. "That's not true. And deep inside you know it. If I wanted to stop you, why would I have flown you all the way to Nepal? I would have simply locked you up in Los Angeles. Or poisoned your food or done one of a million other things. What you're saying doesn't make any sense. You're a good detective. Think about it."

Part of me wanted to push her hands off and fight back. But what she was saying was starting to get through.

I took a long breath. "How did you get here?" I asked, trying desperately to clear my head.

"When I asked the airport official if anyone had arrived in the last day or so, he told me that only one private plane had landed and it had been carrying a Sherpa. His description matched the Sherpa you described in Los Angeles. I dropped Judge Pinkerton's name, and the official gave me a name in return. All I had to do was call information and come here."

It made sense. "Why didn't you just tell me?" I demanded. "Why did you lie to me about what the airport official said to you?"

"Because of something else he said," Maura explained. "I thought it was better not to tell you anything."

"What did he say?"

Maura took a breath. "He told me that someone had died climbing Mount Everest right before we got here."

"My dad!"

"No, it wasn't your dad," she said quickly, trying to keep me from panicking. "It wasn't him. It was a man from Japan. But I wanted to make sure before I mentioned any of this to you and got you worried." She shook her head. "Listen, I'm sorry I didn't tell you. I should have. Maybe I was a little sick with hypoxia, too. But you have to believe me. This man didn't hurt your dad. He wants to help him."

I felt my face flush with embarrassment. "Wow . . ." was all I could say.

"Hey." Maura gave me a smile. "It's okay. It happens to the best of us. I was feeling really out of it myself last night. Most people take at least a few days to go as high as we did. We went way too fast."

She paused to let me catch my breath. Then she said, "Just talk to this man. Hear what he has to say."

I glanced over at the Sherpa who stood a few feet away. He was watching us with a small smile on his face. He certainly didn't look like a criminal mastermind.

"Okay." I walked over to him. "Hello."

"Hello," he said in perfect English. "My name is Darje Jiban."

"You speak English?" I asked him.

"I wasn't sure how to react when you arrived," he explained. "I thought it best if I stalled for time and pretended not to understand English. "

"Do you know where my dad is?"

Jiban looked down. "No, I'm sorry. I wish I did."

My radar told me he was telling the truth. But I still had a million questions. "How do you know him? What were you doing at our house? Why did you have a replica of a human skull?"

Maura held up a hand to cut me off. She indicated I should take a seat with her on one of the two benches that leaned against the side of the house. Jiban swung the other bench around and seated himself so we were facing each other.

"Go ahead, Jiban," Maura directed. "Tell your story."

He nodded and looked at me. "I have been helping your father research a movie script he's writing. It's about famous explorers."

Just by sitting down, I was starting to feel more in control. "How did you meet my dad?"

"That's a long story." He gently smiled. "Let me first tell you about myself. I come from a family of yak farmers. Everyone has always told me that is my job in life. They say I should be happy enough with raising yaks—and not go wandering off to the tops of mountains. But I am the only one in my family who has not climbed Mount Everest. A year ago, on one of his research trips to the area, your father, Henry, heard about my collection."

"What collection?"

"Some people in your country collect baseball cards," he replied. "Here, I collect artifacts and bits of climbing history. Like the climbing axe used by Sir Edmund Hillary and the empty oxygen tank of the first blind climber. Your dad thought looking at my collection could help him write his script. He came to this farm and sat just where you are now. We talked for hours, and we became friends."

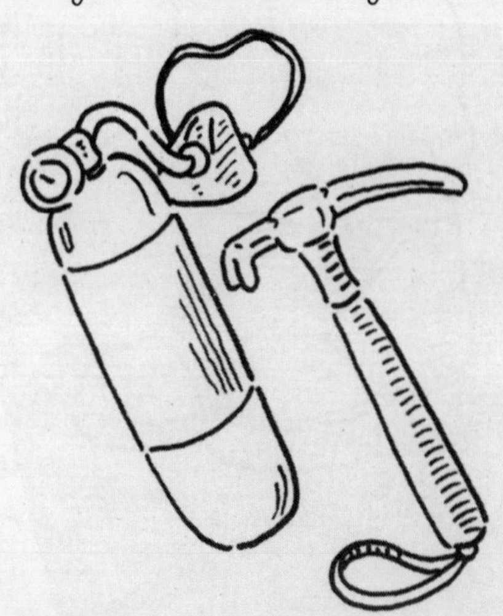

June 6, 2007

I watched his face as he spoke, but still saw no signs of deception. "You took things off the mountain?" I asked.

Jiban looked horrified. "No, of course not. To me, that would be like robbing someone's grave. I believe that when people die on the mountain, all their possessions should remain with them. Do you understand?"

I nodded. It made sense to me. I didn't like it when boat salvage teams took jewels and other personal belongings off shipwrecks where people had died. It seemed disrespectful. I guess this was kind of the same thing.

Jiban was saying, "I acquired these items from auctions and private sales."

"Why did you collect all that stuff?"

"I have this dream to climb the mountain goddess, Mount Everest." His eyes lit up as he spoke.

I asked, "Then why don't you?"

"This." Jiban pointed down at his right leg.

"What?" I couldn't see anything special about it.

He explained, "I was born with one of my legs shorter than the other. It's not a major problem—for a yak farmer. But I let it keep me from climbing. When I told your father about my leg, he put me in touch with Benny Myles. He helped me get a pair of specially designed shoes. And now look!"

JIBAN'S SPECIAL SHOES

June 6, 2007

Jiban was up and walking around. Everything looked smooth, and I couldn't tell that he had ever had a problem.

"Benny Myles sent me boots especially designed for climbing," said Jiban.

"That's just something Uncle Benny would do," I told Maura. "My godfather always wants to make sure that everyone's happy, especially people he works with, like my dad."

Jiban sat back down. "On his last visit to this country, your father told me that he was worried about something. He didn't say what. But he told me that he would call me every evening at nine o'clock my time. If he did not call, he said, that would mean that he was in danger. That meant that I should deliver the skull to you, his son, and repeat the strange phrase—"

"Wonefas nepo," I said.

Jiban nodded. "That's right. I had no idea what it meant. But I trusted your father."

"You flew all the way to Los Angeles to tell me that and throw a skull at me?" I asked.

Jiban explained, "I was already in the city to deliver items to your father that had once belonged to adventurous climbers. It was research for his movie."

"Why didn't you just mail the stuff?"

"Your father believed someone was tampering with his mail. He couldn't prove it, but he did ask me to hand-deliver everything to him personally. I was fine with that—it gave me a chance to meet Benny Myles in person and thank him."

"I wasn't even supposed to be home," I said. "What would you have done if I wasn't there to take the skull from you?"

"I would have waited until you returned," he answered.

"But what does this all mean?" I rubbed a hand over my face, suddenly feeling very, very tired.

"Your father was secretive," Jiban said. "He did not tell me anything more. He explained what I was to do and said that then I should come back home."

"And do what?"

"Once again, he didn't say. I am sorry."

I believed him. And I felt pretty stupid for acting so dumb earlier. But I didn't know how to begin apologizing.

"Now," Jiban said. "Do not move. I insist that you drink some tea and have something to eat. It will make you feel better."

MOUNT EVEREST LOOMING IN THE DISTANCE BEHIND MAURA AND JIBAN

He went inside for a moment and returned with a huge, steaming cup of tea, with plenty of milk and sugar already added. Maura and Jiban sipped from mugs of "chang," a thick, rice-based beer that, according to my guidebook, many Sherpas brew in their homes.

My eyes went to Everest, its peak lost in the clouds. "Do you think he's up there?" I asked.

"I heard talk in Namche Bazar that two men have gone up one of the trickier routes of the mountain without a Sherpa," Jiban said. "One of those men could be your father."

"Well then, that just leaves us one choice," I stated.

"Oh, no," Maura said.

"What is our one choice?" Jiban asked.

"We have to climb Everest."

EVEREST BASE CAMP

June 7, 2007

9:20 PM

Today, I felt like I was back to myself again. After a good night's sleep, I think I finally kicked the altitude sickness.

We spent last night in Base Camp. This was the first stop on the climb up Everest. It's surprising to me that it's not colder here. In the sun, temperatures were in the high forties.

Set on a relatively flat piece of land, Base Camp feels festive. Maybe it's the brightly colored tents that are set up around the huge boulders. Or it could be the prayer flags flapping happily in the breeze that added to the high energy. These flags were put up by Buddhists in the hope that they would help protect the climbers on their journey.

Base Camp is more like a little town than a camp. It has its own doctor, a few trading tents where supplies can be bought, and a communications center with a satellite telephone and Internet access.

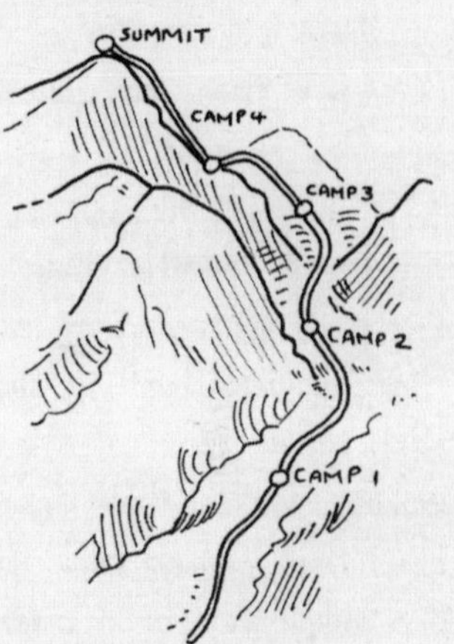

Yesterday, we had tried to reach Judge Pinkerton again. I called Dad's cell phone and even tried sending a note to his e-mail account in case he could somehow check it. I didn't dare say too much in case his e-mails were being intercepted. But I wanted him to know we were close by.

June 7, 2007

Dad,
Don't worry.
We're coming
to get you.
Love,
Nick

Last night, we used Maura's credit card to buy all the climbing gear, tents, oxygen tanks, food, and water that we would need for the climb.

The sun was setting as we wrapped up our shopping. We were leaving one of the supply tents when we ran into a group of Sherpas. They had just returned from the summit. A few of them recognized Jiban and greeted him with surprise. While I couldn't understand what they were saying to him, I heard the Nepali word for "yak" and then "farm."

Jiban's face turned red, and it was obvious they were giving him a hard time.

"I am leading my expedition up Mount Everest tomorrow, and then we'll see who is laughing," Jiban said. He was speaking in English for our benefit.

The other Sherpas just chuckled and shook their heads.

Jiban looked at Maura and me. "I want to ask these FOOLS if they saw your father on the mountain. I will join you in a moment."

Carrying the supplies, Maura and I made our way toward the center of the camp. There must have been thirty or forty climbers and at least twice as many Sherpas. The climbers were bustling about, sharing drinks and toasting each other. Most of them had extremely chapped and raw-looking skin on their faces. While there were quite a few expeditions coming back from the mountain, we were the only one preparing for a climb.

June 7, 2007

In the very middle of the camp, a hand-painted sign was stuck in the ground.

Maura read the sign out loud and then asked me, "Do you know what the words 'because it's there' mean?" It was clear from her tone that she already knew the answer. But I explained anyway.

"It's the answer George Mallory gave when a reporter asked him why he wanted to climb Mount Everest. He said, 'Because it's there.' His answer was so simple and straight-forward it became famous around the world."

Maura nodded. "But Mallory was an experienced mountaineer, an expert—"

"And I'm just a fourteen-year-old kid with no real climbing experience," I interrupted. I could tell that Maura was going to try again to convince me to stay behind, while she and Jiban went up the mountain. "If you have oxygen tanks and a Sherpa who knows what he's doing, you don't have to be a world-class climber. You just have to be in really good shape. And thanks to PDA, we both are."

"I don't think you get how dangerous this is," Maura said. "This isn't a training mission where an instructor gives you a second chance. If you fail up there . . ."

You die. She didn't say the words but they hung in the air between us.

"It's not like we have to make it to the top," I said. "We just have to catch up with my dad and then, we can come back down."

June 7, 2007

"We're not even one hundred percent certain he's up there," Maura said.

Jiban joined us. His face was flushed with excitement. "A Sherpa just told me he spotted two people heading up the mountain as he was coming down. He couldn't tell me much about one of them—even if it was a man or a woman—because the person was too bundled up. But the second person . . . the second person matched the description of your father."

JIBAN MET A SHERPA WHO MIGHT HAVE SEEN DAD!

"Finally, a real lead!" I cried.

"He can't be absolutely sure it was him, but—"

"Was my dad okay?" I cut in eagerly. "Did he look hurt?"

Jiban put a hand on my shoulder. "My friend said the man appeared to be in good health. And that they should be at Camp 1 now."

I looked at my map quickly. "That means they're just a day ahead of us. We can catch up to them!"

June 7, 2007

Jiban said to Maura, "I think we have to consider alerting the authorities. They can send up experienced climbers."

"No," I said immediately. "If whoever took my dad sees a bunch of police coming, he might panic and do something . . . bad. But if there's just the three of us, then we might be able to get close without the kidnapper even noticing. Plus, this could be one of the situations that Judge trained us for."

I waited for Maura's response. She took a second to think things over. "Okay," she agreed. "Tomorrow we climb to Camp 1."

"You want to climb tomorrow?" Jiban asked me. He seemed more than a little worried.

"Yes," I answered.

Jiban looked me in the eye. "Tomorrow is June eighth."

"Oh," I said. Now I understood his anxiety.

"So?" Maura asked. "What's so big about June eighth?"

"On June 8, 1924, George Mallory disappeared on Mount Everest. He was never seen alive again."

Jiban looked at both of us. "Well," he said, "let's hope we have better luck."

IT WAS STILL DARK WHEN WE STARTED OUR CLIMB.

June 8, 2007

8:35 PM

This morning, I started another trek in the middle of the night. But at least this time, I wasn't alone. At 3:30 AM, Jiban, Maura, and I headed out from Base Camp. It was still pitch-dark outside.

The first part of our journey took us from Base Camp to Camp 1. We had to climb only 2,000 feet higher to 19,500 feet above sea level. But we would also have to make our way through the most terrifying part of the climb up Mount Everest. Who knew the trickiest part of the climb was at the beginning?

The Khumbu Icefall sits between the two camps. And it's one of the most beautiful—and frightening—places on the planet. The Icefall is made up of gigantic chunks of ice, some as large as buildings. These chunks are called "seracs," and they are constantly shifting. Gravity pulls them downward about four feet a day.

Hurrying to catch up with my dad and whoever was with him wasn't the only reason we had to get an early start. The seracs pick up speed in the heat of the sun. Huge, seemingly bottomless gaps can quickly open up between them.

Because the seracs are constantly shifting, each year Sherpas establish a new route through the Icefall. They use rope and aluminum ladders laid flat to create bridges over gaps that can be hundreds of feet deep.

As if that wasn't bad enough, our only light came from the moon, the stars, and the lamps on our helmets.

The climb was dangerous and hard. But at least it wasn't so cold!

June 8, 2007

When I commented on the warm weather and clear skies, Jiban smiled. "Don't get used to it, my friend. This time of year the weather is very unpredictable. A storm can develop in the blink of an eye."

TRAGEDY STRIKES TOP OF THE WORLD

—by Holly Fredericks

Climbers Universe August 1996

1996 was the deadliest year in climbing history on the slopes of Mount Everest. While 98 people reached the summit, 15 died trying. That means one person died for about every six that made it to the top. On May 10 alone, eight people were killed when they were caught in a violent storm. One of the climbers who survived that day was Jon Krakauer. He later wrote the bestseller ***Into Thin Air*** about his experience on the mountain.

Jiban was an excellent climber. He showed no signs of being physically challenged, and both Maura and I relied heavily on him to get us through this first part of the climb.

About halfway to Camp 1, we came upon a bridge that was actually made of seventeen ladders. They had been lashed together with rope and spanned the widest, deepest gap yet.

I COULD FEEL THE LADDER MOVING!

June 8, 2007

I kept count as I crawled over each ladder. The hardest part was when I got to the eighth ladder and realized I was right in the middle of the bridge. I could feel it curving slightly from my weight—and for a second I froze. I managed to pull myself together and inched my way over the rest of the gap.

After that horrifying experience, Jiban said that we deserved a break. We took a seat on the edge of the seracs. It felt kind of like a giant but very cold couch.

"So," Maura said, "now that we're on the mountain, how will we find your dad and the other climber?

"Hopefully," I replied, "we'll just catch up to them."

Jiban gestured up toward the summit of Everest. "This is a big mountain. There are many different routes to the top."

I smiled. "But I know which way they'll take."

"How?" Maura asked.

"It all goes back to Mallory and his missing camera. If we retrace Mallory's steps on his last climb, I think we'll find my dad."

Jiban said, "You want to reenact his climb?"

I nodded.

June 8, 2007

"But Mallory died up there," said Maura.

"It's the only chance we have to find my dad." I got to my feet.

Jiban told us break time was over, and we started climbing again.

We made it through the Icefall!

And we made great time, arriving at Camp 1 by 8:45 A.M. Since it was still so early, we decided to keep hiking to the next stop. I'm now in my sleeping bag in my tent at Camp 2.

There's no sign of my dad here. In fact, there is no sign of anyone. We are the only climbers who are headed up the mountain. Jiban says this is very strange. The last few years, more and more people have been making the climb up Everest. There can be twenty or thirty people in this camp at one time, especially this time of year. Where is everyone? The weather still looks clear, but Jiban wonders if other climbers have heard something we haven't—and are staying off the mountain on purpose.

June 8, 2007

But who can worry about the weather now? After more than ten hours of climbing, I'm exhausted!

I was almost too tired to eat but forced myself to stay awake long enough to slurp down the hot beef stew Maura heated on the mini stove. Afterward, I crawled into my tent and am struggling to keep awake long enough to finish this journal ent

WE HAD TO WEAR OXYGEN MASKS AFTER LEAVING CAMP 2.

June 9, 2007

11:45 AM

This morning as we left Camp 2, we reached 21,000 feet above sea level. Up this high, we would become dizzy and grow easily exhausted in the thin air.

Jiban said, "I want you both to put on your oxygen masks and keep them on from now on. I would not want to have our first climb up Chomolungma be our last."

Chomolungma is the Sherpa name for Mount Everest. It means "goddess mother of the world."

You didn't need to tell me twice. I now knew how weird I could get without oxygen. I put on my mask.

Our next destination, Camp 3, is the most dangerous of all the camps. It's halfway up the Lohtse Face, a steep 3,700-foot-high wall of glacial ice. You have to pitch your tents on narrow icy ledges that are totally unprotected from the wind. If a storm were to pop up, we'd have nowhere to go and would have to hunker down with nothing but hope to shield us.

Jiban was looking up at the sky. "I don't like the looks of those clouds," he said, pointing to a dark dusting of clouds off in the distance.

"But we have to go on," I urged. "We're so close now."

Jiban continued to examine the sky for a moment. Then he looked at me. Something in my face seemed to make him change his mind. "Okay," he said. "We can keep climbing. But we must tie ourselves to one another. If a storm does develop, I don't want any of us to get lost."

June 9, 2007

Jiban pulled out a long coil of rope and three clips. We each attached one end of a clip to our waist and the other to the rope. With about 20 feet of rope between each person, Jiban was in the front, then me, and finally, Maura.

"We're gambling a lot on your hunch, Nick," Maura commented as we started to climb again.

"Are you beginning to doubt me?" I asked.

"No," she said with a smile. "I'm just making an observation."

We were climbing for about twenty minutes, making pretty good progress, when the strangest thing happened.

Maura's satellite phone started to ring. Even 40 feet away, Jiban heard it. We both gathered around Maura.

She quickly removed her gloves and oxygen mask. She pulled the phone from her backpack. We were on the side of the world's highest mountain, and Maura was taking a phone call. Bizarre!

"Yes?" she said as she answered the phone. After a moment, her green eyes flashed with excitement. "Hello, Judge Pinkerton."

Judge! I felt a wave of relief wash over me.

Maura spoke into the phone. "Yes, ma'am, well, it's a long story. Yes, he's right here, let me put him on."

I pushed up my oxygen mask as I took the phone from Maura.

"Judge?" I said.

"Nick! Are you okay?" The connection was almost completely filled with static, but her voice was the best thing I'd heard in days.

"Yes, we're fine. I—"

Our voices were overlapping from the bad connection. Judge spoke quickly as if she knew we might be cut off at any second. "I finished my investigation and got your messages about your father still being missing. We've been able to triangulate your location by zeroing in on Maura's satellite phone. I know exactly where you are, and I'm sending assistance. Go back to Camp 2 and wait there. Did you hear me, Nick?"

"Yes, Judge," I said, "but—"

"Nick? Did you hear me?" her words were almost drowned by static. "Nick, if—"

And then her voice was gone. I looked down at Maura's satellite phone. There was no signal.

I gave the phone back to Maura and told her and Jiban what Judge had said. "She wants us to go back to Camp 2. She says help is on the way."

"All right," Jiban said, looking up at the sky. "I cannot argue with that. The storm I feared is now most certainly on its way. We must be very careful."

June 9, 2007

And he was right.

About five minutes later, as we were heading back down to Camp 2, the storm hit. It was almost like I had blinked and, suddenly, we were in the middle of a blizzard. I imagined that this was what it must be like to be lost in thick, dark smoke. At its thickest, I couldn't see more than a few inches in any direction.

Somehow, I got spun around, and the rope that connected us wrapped itself around my shins. I couldn't walk. And yet Jiban was still pulling on the line.

I unclipped myself from the rope for a second so that I could untangle myself—and then I fell.

The rope slithered out of my hands.

I called out, but I could barely hear my own voice.

I tried to retrace my steps but realized they were already covered in snow.

The wind screamed around me, and the snow felt like carpenter's nails on the part of my face that wasn't protected by my goggles or oxygen mask. There hadn't been time to put on my ski mask.

I was in serious trouble.

Find shelter! I screamed at myself.

But where?

There! There was a rock face that might protect me. I walked over to it—and through it. It hadn't been a rock face, after all, but an illusion created by the blowing snow.

I turned to go back and fell again.

This time, I skittered down the icy slope directly toward the edge of a cliff. I felt my oxygen mask tear off my face, and it was gone.

I tried everything, but I couldn't slow myself down—I

was going to plummet over the side. And that would mean certain death—

My feet shot over the edge—

And a hand reached out of nowhere and grabbed my arm. I had been moving with such speed that my body swung out and back onto the cliff.

I looked up at my savior.

I expected to see Jiban or Maura. . . .

But it was a man wearing a bright red down jacket and matching red snow pants. His face was nearly hidden under the red cap and snow goggles he wore. But in an instant, I recognized him anyway.

It was my godfather! It was Uncle Benny!

I COULDN'T BELIEVE UNCLE BENNY WAS HERE!

June 9, 2007

3:50 PM

In my shock, I decided the hypoxia must be back and stronger than before.

What was Uncle Benny doing here on top of Mount Everest? Who would I see next? My third-grade teacher strolling down the mountainside?

I rubbed my eyes, trying to see if the vision would clear.

Uncle Benny let out a loud laugh. "Kid, you're not dreaming!" he shouted over the howling wind. "It's me standing with you here at the top of the world."

I glanced quickly around. More like dangling from the top of the world. We were on a narrow ledge that was covered with ice. On one side, just behind me, was the cliff that had almost taken my life. On the other side, a rock outcropping about the size of a minivan jutted into the air behind Uncle Benny.

I gaped at him. "Uncle Benny?"

"In the flesh," he bellowed. "What the heck are you doing up here, kid?"

"I'm so glad to see you!" I cried. "I'm looking for Dad. Did he come to Everest with you?"

Uncle Benny nodded and said more quietly, "Yes."

"Where is he?" I demanded.

"Your dad wanted to come here to research his script." Uncle Benny crouched down so he was closer to me. "I came along to help. He figured you wouldn't be home for another week or so. He didn't want you to worry about him climbing up here, so he decided not to tell you that he was going."

June 9, 2007

That sounded really strange.

"Where is he?" I asked again.

Uncle Benny shook his head. "We almost reached the top. We were about 2,000 feet below the summit . . ."

"Right where George Mallory's body was found."

"What's that?" Benny asked me.

I realized that I must have spoken out loud. I was still feeling a little dizzy, and the buzzing was back in my head. I tried to focus all my attention on Uncle Benny. He continued, "When the storm kicked up, we decided we'd have to reach the summit another day. We started to make our way down, and . . ." His voice trailed off.

"And . . . ?" I prodded, almost not wanting him to answer. "And what?"

Tears filled Uncle Benny's eyes. "Your dad . . . ," he said. "Your dad is missing. It was stupid of us to climb up here without a Sherpa."

"What do you mean MISSING?" I could barely form the words.

For a second, he said nothing. The wind whipped against us, stinging us with icy snow. Finally, he spoke. "Kid, I'm afraid that your dad is gone."

"GONE?" I was horror-struck.

He lifted up his goggles so I could see his face. "He got lost in the storm. And I don't think there's any hope of finding him."

Other kids might have burst into tears, started shouting, or maybe even fainted.

But I was too busy watching Uncle Benny's face. Even if I was having a tough time breathing, my detective radar was apparently still functioning. "What did you say?" I said, keeping an eye on his every move.

"Your dad is somewhere out there. Lost."

There! Uncle Benny's lower eyelids reddened and his brows lifted ever so slightly. I doubt many people would have even noticed these changes, but my mind zeroed in on them.

"Why are you lying?" I asked him.

And it was like watching a deer freeze in the headlights.

Uncle Benny stared at me. "Oh, kid, now why would you say something like that?"

"Because you're not telling the truth," I said.

"The truth about what?" He put his goggles back over his face.

"I don't know," I replied. "But I do know that my dad didn't get lost up on this mountain—"

And that's when Uncle Benny rushed at me, his arms out.

Was he going to push me over?

My body reacted before I could even think about it. I jumped to the side and fell to the ground—just as his gloved hands landed on my shoulder.

June 9, 2007

I grabbed at the slick ice as he yanked on my jacket, but there was nothing for me to hold onto. "No!" I shouted. Maybe it was my terror-filled voice that caused him to stop.

For whatever reason, Benny suddenly pulled away. I lay on the ground near the cliff, out of breath and terrified.

Benny's sudden violence seemed to have startled even himself. He took another step away from me, holding up his hands as if to say he meant no harm. He plopped down on the nearby rock outcropping, using part of it like a chair. I pushed myself up into a sitting position. We looked at each other, breathing heavily.

Without a word, Benny reached into his pack and took out his oxygen tank. He placed the mask over his face and breathed deeply.

UNCLE BENNY KEPT THE OXYGEN MASK.

I eyed the oxygen with real hunger. Altitude sickness was striking. My earlier hypoxia attack was nothing compared to this. My vision was blurry, and I felt disoriented. I was so sleepy, I could barely hold my head up and had to fight to stay alert. If I didn't get oxygen soon, my body would begin to shut down.

Finally, Benny removed the mask. "I thought that I could get you to believe me. I guess there's a reason I'm a producer and not an actor."

"Why did you kidnap my dad?" My voice sounded like an empty gasp. I was surprised he could even hear me.

"Oh, kid, I feel bad about all this," he said. "You know, I was the one who came up with the idea for making a movie about Sir Edmund Hillary's famous climb. My last few movies have flopped, but this one, this one is going to be different. Your dad helped me out with the research. And then, always the detective"— he spat this last word as if it were something disgusting—"he decides he has to find Mallory's camera to discover the real truth!"

I couldn't believe what I was hearing. "All this is about a stupid movie?"

"IT'S NOT STUPID!" he suddenly screamed at me. His face flashed with rage, and I thought he might attack me again. But then he seemed to get his emotions under control. He chuckled bitterly. "Well, one thing was stupid. Very stupid. I named the movie HILLARY: FIRST TO THE TOP. Can you believe it? I poured millions of dollars into that movie—every last dime I had."

"So what?" I wasn't getting any of this. I just wanted to find my dad.

His frustration boiled to the surface. "Didn't you hear me? The movie is called HILLARY: **FIRST** TO THE TOP! And your dad is trying to find Mallory's camera that could show Hillary wasn't first. No one wants to see HILLARY: **SECOND** TO THE TOP. I'll be completely wiped out if this movie tanks."

"I don't understa—" I couldn't finish my sentence. I was sucking at the air like a goldfish that's been dumped out of its bowl.

But it didn't matter. Uncle Benny seemed to have almost forgotten that I was there. He ranted on. "That film could show Mallory standing at the peak of Everest. That would make my movie the world's biggest joke!"

"Just . . . change . . . title," I sputtered.

He gave a fake laugh. "Ha! Well, thanks for that idea," he said sarcastically. "It's too late to change the title. A huge star has signed a contract to play Hillary. If I change his character to Mallory, I'll have to pay him double. Posters are made, action figures are being sold, ads have appeared. . . . I can't back out now." He was almost screaming. "Everything—my money, my reputation—is on the line! If Mallory's camera exists, it must be destroyed!"

Uncle Benny suddenly stopped ranting. He looked at me with tears in his eyes. Real ones, this time. "You're my godson. Without thinking, I saved you from falling over that cliff . . ." After a pause, Benny added, "And that might have been a mistake."

I felt a chill unlike any other in my heart.

"What are . . . you . . . going to do?" I stammered.

"Do you think I'm going to hurt you? Ah, kid! I'm not going to hurt you," he said in a soothing voice. "You're exhausted and you're not thinking straight. I'll tell you what. Why don't you close your eyes and rest for a second? Then we'll figure out what to do about your dad, okay?"

"No! Not okay!" I tried to yell. But my words came out slurred, like, "Na, nah okay."

Uncle Benny smiled as if I had agreed to the plan. He put the oxygen mask back on his face and watched me.

He was right. I was feeling more and more sleepy. Without oxygen, my body was literally closing down.

I craved sleep like I'd crave a turkey dinner on Thanksgiving.

But a voice in the back of my head told me that if I closed my eyes, I might never open them again.

I would sleep forever. And that might be exactly what Uncle Benny wanted.

I struggled to my feet.

"Sit down, kid," Benny said gently. And when I didn't do as he asked, his voice became as cold as the wind. "I said, sit down."

But I stayed on my feet. Well, kind of. I wobbled back and forth, teetering close to the edge of the cliff.

He watched me, waiting for me to fall. But I managed to stagger a few steps away from the edge as if I was going to walk past him.

Benny stood up quickly and reached out for my arm.

I called on my remaining strength and spun away. When I wasn't there for him to grab, Benny lost his balance.

His arms pinwheeled in the air for a moment—and then he went down. His head smacked against the rock protrusion—hard—and his body was still.

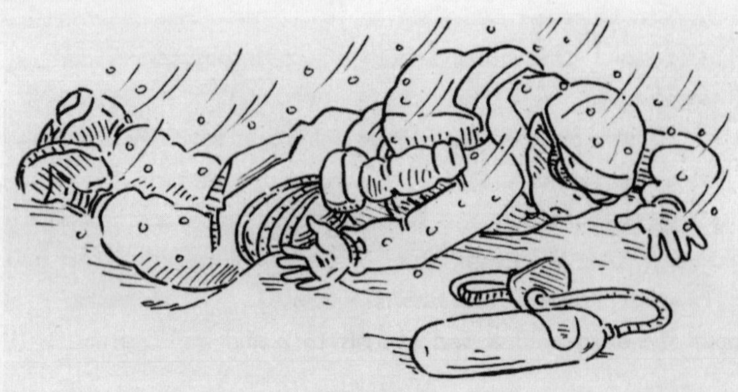

I waited a moment before moving again.

Was this a trick?

After a few seconds, he still hadn't moved. Benny had knocked himself out.

I inched my way over to him and grabbed the oxygen mask that was lying next to him. I greedily put it over my face and sucked in oxygen. I could feel my lungs opening up like flowers in the sun. The pain in my chest eased, and the stars in my vision began to recede.

"Much better," I said out loud.

Now what was I going to do?

I looked down at Benny. He had a coil of rope attached to his belt. I removed the rope and hog-tied his hands and feet. I heard him moaning and realized that I had tied him up just in time.

Then I heard the moan again.

It wasn't coming from Benny.

I strained to listen. The noise was coming from the other side of the rock outcropping.

Someone was over there. And it sounded like that someone was hurt.

I placed the oxygen mask back over Benny's face and went to investigate.

When I came around the corner, I spotted my dad immediately.

He was propped up against the rock, which had protected him from the most severe effects of the blizzard. There was a gag in his mouth, and his hands and feet were tied. An oxygen tank and mask sat on a supply sled about 2 feet away from him, too far for him to reach.

"Dad!" I shouted and rushed to him.

June 9, 2007

I carefully removed the gag from his mouth.

"Hi, Nick," he said with that toothy grin of his. "I see you got my message."

I FOUND DAD TIED UP AND GAGGED!

I WAS SO HAPPY DAD WAS OKAY!

June 9, 2007

5:15 PM

I untied my dad, grabbed the oxygen mask, and handed it to him.

Grinning all the while, he breathed in oxygen, and his color started to return to normal.

He held out his arms to me, and we hugged for a long time.

My eyes filled with tears, and when I pulled away, I saw Dad's eyes were shiny with tears, as well.

"Where's Benny?" he asked me.

Quickly, I told him about how I'd come up the mountain with Maura and Jiban. And about my struggle with Benny, and that he was tied up on the other side of the rock.

His eyes had widened with fear as I recounted my story. But now they were filled with pride. "Outstanding job, Nick," he said as he squeezed my gloved hand in his. "You've done incredible work."

Even though he'd been breathing in the oxygen and was now sitting up, Dad still looked exhausted and beat up. But I couldn't resist starting in with a question. "Okay, here's what I've been wanting to ask for days: What. Is. Going. On?"

Dad chuckled. "Sounds like you've worked it out already. Here's the short version: I was working on that screenplay with Benny. I couldn't let go of the idea that Mallory might have been the first to climb to the summit. I started to hunt for his camera. When Benny realized my research could destroy his movie, he warned me to back off, but . . ." He shrugged with a sheepish smile.

"But you couldn't let it go," I finished for him.

Nodding, Dad said, "Benny came to the house, kidnapped me at gunpoint, and forced me to come to Everest with him. Once we left the house, he told me he'd come after you if I didn't do exactly as he said. Benny wanted me to use my knowledge of Mallory to find the camera. Then he would destroy it, and his movie would be safe."

The thought of Benny pulling a gun on my dad made my stomach clench. "It's still hard to believe Uncle Benny would do all this!"

"I know," said my dad. "He used to be such a good guy. I guess the pressure of possibly losing everything finally got to him."

MAURA FOUND US.

"But what about the timing?" A voice said behind me. I turned, and Maura was there.

"Maura!" I cried, and got to my feet.

She came over to me and put her arm around my shoulders. "I'm so glad to see you, Nick."

"Me, too," I agreed and turned to my dad. "This is Maura."

"I know." Dad smiled at her. "We met last time I was at PDA."

"Where's Jiban?" I asked Maura.

"After you unclipped, we got separated looking for you," she replied. "I'm sure he'll be fine. The worst of the storm has passed, and the skies are already clearing." She looked at my dad. "You have no idea how hard your son worked to find you, sir."

DAD SMILED AT MAURA.

Blushing, I said, "Maura's right, Dad. I mean, about the timing. How did you have time to set up all the clues for me in Los Angeles?"

Dad nodded, as if he had expected this question. "Ever since I told Benny I wanted to find Mallory's camera, my detective radar had been telling me that things weren't quite right. I could feel that something sinister was going on. For one thing, someone was tampering with my mail. I was worried. I planted the clues in our office and told Jiban what to do if he didn't hear from me at the regular time we set."

"How did you know to tell me to come to Everest?" I wondered. "How could you be sure that you'd be kidnapped and brought here?"

He shook his head. "I didn't know. At that point, I wasn't even completely sure Benny was a bad guy—or at least I didn't want to believe it. The clues were supposed to show you that if I had an 'accident' or disappeared, it probably had something to do with Mallory's camera. I didn't think you'd follow them all the way to Everest!"

Now I was starting to understand. "So you had the clues all ready when Uncle Benny nabbed you?"

"That's right," Dad said. "I'd set them up two weeks ago. Then the day of the kidnapping, I spotted Benny lurking outside our office window. He was activating a cell-phone jammer to block any calls for help I might have made."

PRIVATE CELL-PHONE JAMMERS LIKE THIS ONE ARE ILLEGAL IN THE UNITED STATES!

ENGLISH SPY CLUB MAGAZINE • 24

SUPER JAMMER!

Tired of sitting on the train listening to people chat on their mobiles while you're trying to read the newspaper? You need Super Jammer, the battery-powered device that blocks mobile phone calls. It transmits signals that collide with and cancel the mobile's signals—making the phone useless!

That's why I hadn't been able to reach him from the plane after I left PDA, I thought.

Dad continued, "Benny was heading inside the house and I knew I had limited time to act."

Maura asked, "Why didn't you just write a note?"

"Benny might have found it and destroyed it. I had to leave a message that only a detective could find. I pricked my own finger and left a drop of blood on the MP3 player, and then quickly set up the clock on the floor. Everything else was already set up in case of just such an emergency." My dad looked at me. "I knew you would unravel the clues and solve the mystery!"

Dad was smiling, but he shuddered. He was getting too cold. It was time to get him off this mountain. Together, Maura and I helped him to his feet.

As he was brushing the snow off his down parka, I said, "Too bad you couldn't find the camera."

Dad smiled. And there was something about that smile . . .

I gazed at him. "No!" I cried in disbelief.

"What?" Maura asked, looking at me and then my dad. "What's going on?"

As if to answer her, my dad took off one glove and reached into the pocket of his jacket very carefully. When he removed his hand again, he was holding something up for us to see.

It was a camera. Mallory's camera, to be specific.

DAD HAD MALLORY'S CAMERA!

My dad explained that the camera was actually about 750 feet uphill from where Mallory's body was discovered. A few years earlier, there were rumors that a Sherpa had found a pen near that spot with the date 1923 and the inscription "To my darling George" on it. Why might a lost pen indicate that a camera was nearby? This Vest Pocket B had a special feature. It allowed someone to write an inscription directly onto the film through a little window in the back of camera. Dad determined that the pen was out because Mallory was writing something either in a notebook . . . or on the camera itself. Since no notebook was discovered, my dad decided there was a fifty-fifty chance that the camera was near where the pen was discovered.

"I always wanted to see if my hunch was correct," Dad said. "And Benny kidnapping me gave me a chance to find out. When we were on a ridge above the spot where the pen had been found, I acted like I had a cramp. I faked a collapse and rolled down the slope. By the time Benny got down to me, I had found the camera and tucked it into my coat without him noticing. Then I pretended to help him look for the camera. After a few hours, Benny gave up, and we headed back down the mountain. When the blizzard started, he decided he didn't need me anymore. He tied me up and left me here. He never knew I'd found the camera."

Dad had it—the camera that could answer one of the world's greatest mysteries.

HOW TO DEVELOP REALLY OLD FILM

If you find a roll of film that's been frozen for more than fifty years, what should you do? Try this!

1. CHILL OUT
Keep the film frozen until just before you develop it. Otherwise, it might fall apart when it thaws.

2. TAKE THE TEST
Cut off a tiny piece of film from the end of the roll. Use it to test your development method before you risk the entire roll.

3. DON'T RUSH!
This isn't a project for a "One-Hour Photomat." Take your time.

DAD HUGGED JIBAN.

"Why, Henry Fitzmorgan!" Jiban called out. He had just come around the rock outcropping.

"Jiban, my friend!" Dad cried. He gently handed me the camera and rushed to Jiban. My dad threw his arms around him.

The Sherpa looked embarrassed for a second but then returned the hug wholeheartedly.

"I can't believe we found you," Jiban said.

"I can," Dad said, pulling back from Jiban so he could look him in the eye. "Thank you for everything."

Jiban appeared embarrassed again and looked down.

I told Jiban and Maura about what had happened with Uncle Benny. When I was finished, Dad turned to me. "Nick," he said, "what are you thinking of doing with the camera?"

I gazed down at the incredible object in my hands. This camera had been up on this mountain for more than eighty years, and yet it looked as good as new.

I thought about what Jiban had said about leaving things on the mountain. That to take a dead person's property off the mountain was like robbing his or her grave.

"We have to do what we can to protect George Mallory's final resting place," I finally said. "The camera should stay up here."

Dad's face broke out into a new grin. "Bully for you, as Judge would say." He clapped me on the back. "I agree with you a hundred percent. I guess we've solved enough cases to know that some mysteries are best left unsolved. To honor the memory of Mallory, we'll put the camera back where I found it."

"But you're way too beat up, Dad," I said. "You can't make that climb again."

"I'll do it," Jiban volunteered. He was smiling. "I'm happy to return the camera. After that, I'll continue on to the summit and fulfill my lifelong dream of climbing this mountain goddess."

Before he left, Jiban helped himself to supplies from the sled that Uncle Benny had left near my dad. When he was loaded up with extra oxygen tanks and water, we all gathered around him.

JIBAN TOOK MALLORY'S CAMERA.

I handed him Mallory's camera, which he carefully put into his pack.

"Well, I guess this is good-bye," I said sadly. "Thank you for everything, Jiban."

The Sherpa looked offended. "What is this good-bye, Henry? Doesn't your son know that friends don't say good-bye, they say see you soon?"

Jiban laughed. He grabbed me in a quick hug and then gave one to Maura and finally, to my dad. Without another word, he turned and strode off up toward the peak.

"Good luck!" Maura called after him.

Now it was just the three of us. It was time to get back to Camp 2.

"As tempting as it is," my dad said, "there's one thing I guess we shouldn't leave up here. . . ."

"What?" I asked.

"Your godfather."

It was a bad joke, but I had to smile. I even caught Maura wearing a little grin.

We dragged the supply sled around the rock where Uncle Benny was still unconscious but breathing fine. We strapped him to the sled. Even if it tipped upside down, he wouldn't fall off. That should keep him safe until we reached Camp 2, where Judge would have help waiting for us.

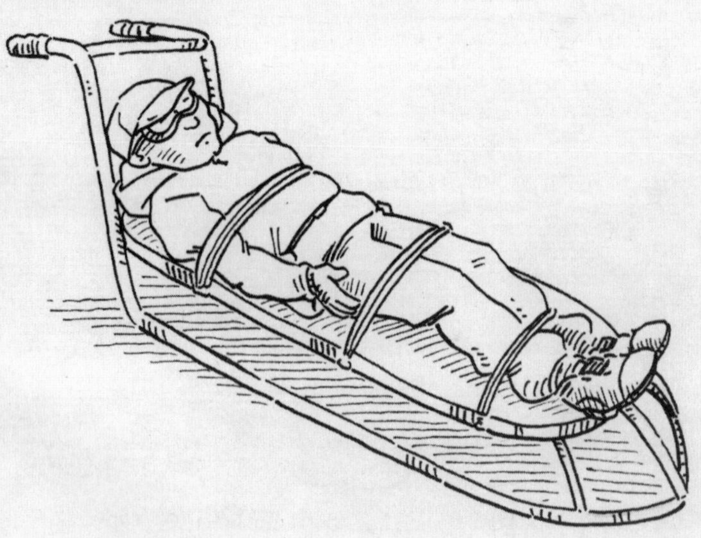

June 9, 2007

As we headed down the mountain, I paused to look up toward the peak once more. I could just barely make out Jiban. He was a dark silhouette as he strode confidently toward the top.

JIBAN WAVED TO US AND KEPT CLIMBING.

As if he could sense our eyes on him, he turned and waved. Then, he began climbing again and soon disappeared into the clouds.

We had cracked a big case here today, but the mountain looked just as mysterious as ever.

Dad had paused next to me, following my gaze. "We'll come back someday and make it all the way to the top, okay?"

I put an arm around his shoulder. "I think I've gone far enough for a while," I said.

He smiled, and the four of us headed down the mountain together.

WARNING: This message gives away parts of the story!

A NOTE FROM THE AUTHOR

One of the fun things about being a writer is that I can send my characters to places I've always dreamed of going. At least until I have the chance to make my dreams come true in person, that is.

Just about everyone I know has imagined climbing Mount Everest at one time or another. So when I was thinking up places to take detective Nick Fitzmorgan, it seemed like the perfect spot. Not only because it's the world's tallest mountain but also because it's home to one of history's greatest mysteries: Was George Mallory the first climber to reach the summit?

To make this fascinating mystery even more exciting, I took a few liberties. For instance, Mallory was lost while climbing up the north side of Everest. I wanted Nick to cross the dangerous Khumbu Icefall so I sent him and his friends up the south side.

And, as far as I know, Mallory's camera has never been discovered. Its location is a mystery just waiting to be solved! Will you be the one to crack the case?

Yours in time,

Bill Doyle

WHERE IS JUDGE?

PASSPORT

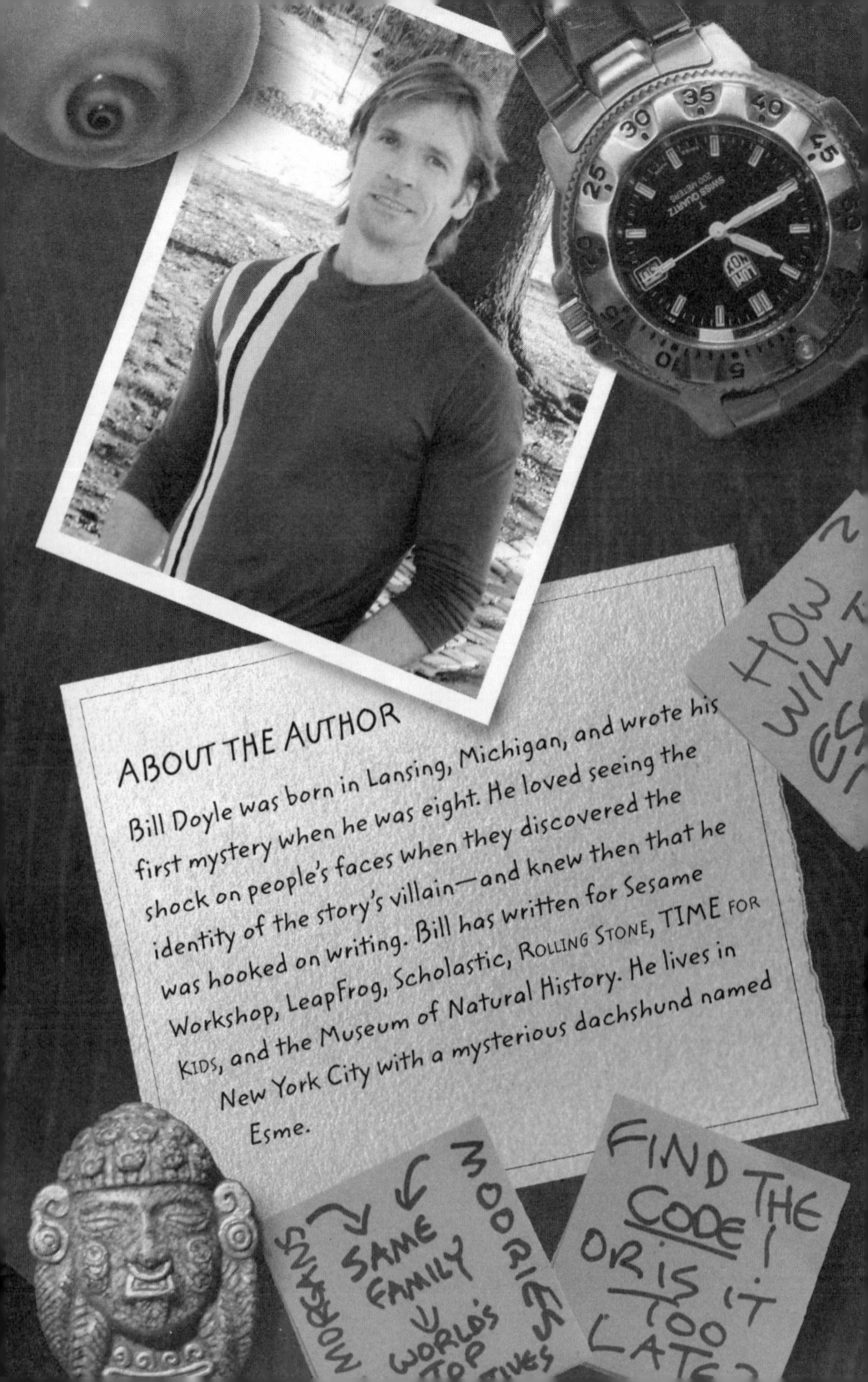

ABOUT THE AUTHOR

Bill Doyle was born in Lansing, Michigan, and wrote his first mystery when he was eight. He loved seeing the shock on people's faces when they discovered the identity of the story's villain—and knew then that he was hooked on writing. Bill has written for Sesame Workshop, LeapFrog, Scholastic, Rolling Stone, TIME for Kids, and the Museum of Natural History. He lives in New York City with a mysterious dachshund named Esme.

Check out these other gripping Crime Through Time™ books!

Now in stores!

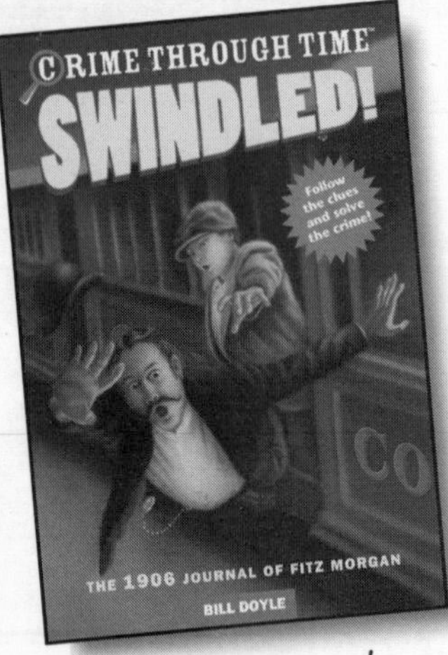

Now in stores!

Now in stores!

2007 Edition

THE INSPECTOR

$1.00 We Have an "EYE" for News

MYSTERY
ON TOP OF THE WORLD

KATHMANDU, NEPAL: Two weeks ago, six climbers went up Mount Everest, determined to put to rest an 83-year-old mystery. "We searched for evidence that could tell us if George Mallory was first to reach the top of Everest," says Troy Howard, the leader of the climbers. "Unfortunately, we didn't find what we were looking for."

In 1953, Sir Edmund Hillary and Tenzing Norgay became the first to officially summit Everest. However, some people believe that Englishman George Mallory was the first climber to make it to the top of the world's tallest mountain. In 1924, Mallory was making his third attempt to climb Everest. While it is certain that Mallory died on the mountain, no one knows exactly when. Did he die before or after he had reached the summit? If Mallory died after he reached the top, he would have beaten Hillary by almost 30 years.

Many experts believe that the answer to the mystery lies inside a camera that Mallory was carrying when he died. If he took a picture of himself at the top, the film inside the camera would show that photo. It would be the proof Howard is looking for to show that Mallory made it to the summit first. But, to this day, no one has been able to find Mallory's camera.

"Still," Howard says, "I'm not going to give up. This mystery is just too important to be left unsolved."

A camera like Mallory's

News

Giving a Face to the Dead

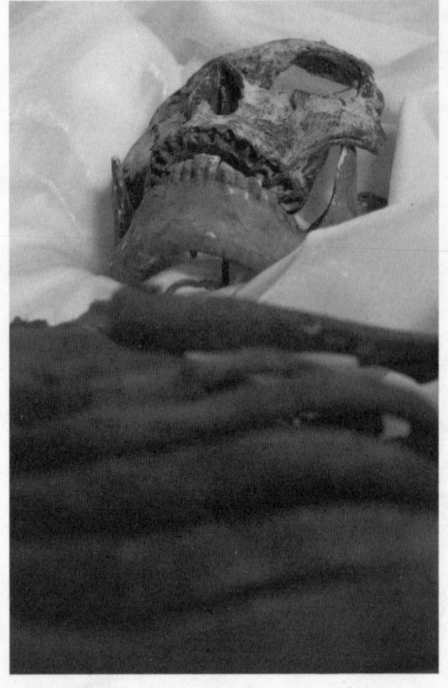

IRON CITY, MI: Three campers recently discovered a human skull in the woods near Iron City. Scientists determined that the skull was from a male adult and that it had been in the woods for 25 to 35 years. But in that 10-year time, there were reports of 134 missing men in Michigan. So to whom did the skull belong?

To answer that question, local officials called in Keith Colwin, a forensics expert with degrees in art history and computer science. He uses these areas of his education to reconstruct the faces of unidentified skulls. If a face looks enough like the person did when alive, someone may be able to make an ID.

Colwin warns that the skull found in the Michigan woods might never be identified. "Facial reconstruction isn't as easy as they make it look on TV," he says. "It isn't an exact science."

Colwin points out that a skull doesn't give many clues as to what soft-tissue features, like a nose and a mouth, might have looked like. And it won't give any information about hair color, facial hair, scars, or tattoos, or whether a person might have worn glasses. "The person doing the reconstruction must be experienced enough to make well-educated guesses," Colwin says.

While some facial reconstruction experts use computer programs to rebuild faces, Colwin prefers to work with his own two hands. He uses clay to slowly build the layers of a face on the skull. "I'm not convinced the software is up to the task yet," says Colwin. "That might change in the next year or two, thanks to new technology."

Colwin is nearly finished rebuilding the face on the Michigan skull. When he's done, the police will run a photo of it in newspapers. "If I've done my job well," Colwin says, "someone may recognize the face as a missing family member or friend."

Entertainment

Stay in Control

REDMOND, WA: Nintendo has a way to make sure that you don't starve while gaming. Their one-handed controller means you'll have one hand free to munch on popcorn and other game-time snacks. The device has motion and position sensors. If you're playing a tennis game, you can just swing or flick the controller, and the racquet on the screen will mirror every movement you make!

DREAM TAKES WING

SEATTLE, WA: The Wright brothers would be floored! The new 787 Dreamliner is probably unlike anything they ever imagined. This airplane carries up to 296 passengers but uses 20 percent less fuel and produces 20 percent fewer emissions than similarly sized aircraft. Inside, the passengers say they're more comfortable than they are on other airplanes. Wireless Internet connections provide entertainment, and added humidity in the cabin air reduces the number of headaches and cases of airsickness as well. Plus—the views! Windows on the Dreamliner are as much as 70 percent bigger than those on other planes.

READY TO BE A CYBORG?

More than 2,000 people around the world have had computer microchips implanted in their body. The chips contain information that could save their lives. Equipped with a radio transmitter about the size of a grain of rice, the chip holds a 16-digit personal ID number. In an emergency, doctors can scan the chip, get the ID number, and find out information about the patient from a computer database. This works especially well if the patient is too sick to talk and cannot tell doctors about his or her medical history. But it's not all for medical reasons. The same technology is being used to help owners find lost pets that have the implanted chips.

"IS THERE AN ANTEATER ON MY HEAD?"

ARMONK, NY: Thanks to IBM's brand-new Multilingual Automatic Speech-to-Speech Translator (MASTOR), questions like these won't be a problem—even if you're in a country where you don't speak the language. Imagine you're in Peru and want to know where to find a zoo to drop off your anteater. All you have to do is speak into the device in English and press a button. MASTOR will translate what you say and repeat it in Spanish, Quechua, or Aymara to whoever is within earshot. And when someone responds by speaking into the device—MASTOR will change his or her words from Spanish to English automatically.

Sports

On the Ball

CHICAGO, IL: She's the two-time Yugoslav national table tennis champ. And now Biljana Golic is looking to conquer the world and make table tennis as popular as tennis played on a court! Even when male fans wave signs proposing marriage to her during matches, this champion stays focused on her game. Go, Golic!

She's Got Drive

WILBRAHAM, MA: Watch out, Danica! Wilbraham's own Erin Crocker is looking to be the next big NASCAR star. She's been racing since she was seven years old and was the first woman to win the World of Outlaws sprint-car race. Crocker not only has guts—she's also got brains. She graduated with an industrial and management engineering degree from Rensselaer Polytechnic Institute.

Travel

Mickey Mouse on Everest?

ORLANDO, FL: The Walt Disney World Resort is betting on the public's endless fascination with Mount Everest. They have created a new ride called Expedition Everest. Passengers climb aboard a roller coaster that looks like an old mountain railway. The train travels through bamboo forests, past splashing waterfalls, along sparkling glacier fields, and climbs up to snow-capped peaks. But passengers will be shocked when the track suddenly ends! In a flash, the railway cars are tossed forward and backward through mountain caverns and icy canyons—and finally, race passengers to a showdown with the mysterious abominable snowman!

ASK DR. NOITALL

Dear Dr. Noitall,

Where can I grab hot trends in fashion without blowing tons of cash?

Confused About Clothes

Dear Confused,
Try your attic! That's right. Clothes that your parents might have boxed up years ago could be your key to catwalk cool. Normally about 20 years pass from the time a clothing trend goes out of style to when it comes back full force. Retro could be your future! Look for those oversized, "ugly" sweaters from the late 80s—they could be making comeback any day now!